Domestic Violence The Disease

The Sara Farraday Story

By: Annette Reid

ISBN: 1463746318
ISBN-13: 9781463746315
Library of Congress Control Number: 2011912932
CreateSpace, North Charleston, SC

Foreword

This story is about a disease. It has the ability to strike at any time. Young or old, black or white, its signs and symptoms do not discriminate. It can be fatal if you don't find a cure for yourself. A liar is someone who fills your head with negative thoughts and lowers your self-esteem. A manipulator, who can make you feel embarrassed to talk to other people, including your own family. This story is fiction, but the events are based on true episodes that took place. The young lady in the story, Sara Farraday, was one of the lucky ones. Her struggles will take her down a path filled with deception, mystery, and murder. She finally got her life back on track after several years of abuse. She and her family were victims of domestic violence. She overcame this disease, but not before it almost destroyed the lives of her and her children. I encourage anyone, no matter who you are, if you are in a domestic violence situation, please get help. Will you find the light that so many people desperately seek, or will you continue to wander around in sheer darkness? Find the light, if not for yourself, then at least for your children and any other loved ones who might be at risk of falling prey to this sickness. Don't let this disease go on without a cure.

CHAPTER ONE:

The Nightmare

If you could turn back the hands of time, would you change your life for the better, or would you just continue to make more mistakes and regrets? As I sat in my six-by-eight jail cell, all I could do was think about holding my son and telling him how much I love him. How could I have been so stupid? It was my fault. All I ever wanted was the perfect family.

I'd been in jail now for twenty days, but it seemed more like twenty years. There was a smell of urine in the air. The room was dark and gray. No windows to see the bright sunshine. It reminded me of an extremely cloudy day. I was there by myself in solitary confinement. The judge said that I would be safer in solitary confinement. I was not allowed to go outside with the other ladies. I showered when everyone else had gone back to their cells. The guards were there, but I only saw them when they brought my meals. Reading books was my only source of entertainment.

No matter how many times you say you are innocent, you've already been found guilty and sentenced by the other inmates. I was guilty, but not of what they arrested me for. I was guilty of almost destroying the lives of my children and myself. I became prey to a disease called domestic violence.

My husband Mike had been drinking again as usual. He really went out of control this time. He grabbed my neck and started choking me as hard as he could. I literally saw the flames of hell in his eyes. I thought for sure he was going to kill me this time. My four-year-old son, Michael Jr., grabbed onto his father and bit his leg. Mike turned around and slapped him as hard as he could. Michael Jr. fell and accidentally hit the back of his head on the edge of the kitchen table.

When he went down to the floor, the only thing I could see was my baby boy lying in a pool of blood. It all happened so fast. I couldn't do anything to stop him from falling. Mike turned around and looked at me.

"It's all your fault, Sara. See what you made me do."

By that time, I had grabbed a knife off the kitchen counter. When Mike walked toward me again, I took the knife and cut the top of his hand. I told him if he ever touched me again, I'd kill him.

I heard sirens. They were loud. The neighbors had probably heard all the commotion and called the police. I ran over to check on my son. He was so lifeless and still. I didn't know if he was dead or alive. I started to scream for help.

The police came to the door and kicked it open. They called an ambulance for little Michael. They told me not to move him because they didn't know how serious his injuries were. I covered him with a blanket.

When the police asked what happened, I told them what took place at the house. It was evident that Mike had been drinking. He kept screaming out that it was my fault. He told them that I pushed Michael Jr. on the floor.

"See, look at me. That crazy woman tried to stab me with a knife." He just kept screaming, "She's crazy!" The police took him out the door and placed him in the backseat of the police car.

I kept calling Michael Jr.'s name, but he did not say a word. He just lay there with his eyes closed. The ambulance finally arrived. That was the longest five minutes of my life. They said that his pulse was weak, and he had lost a lot of blood. They immediately took him to the hospital. I rode along in the ambulance, still in shock from everything that had just taken place.

We arrived at the emergency room within a couple of minutes. The doctor said that he had injured his head, causing swelling to his brain. They could not operate at this time until the swelling went down. He had no other choice but to keep Michael Jr. in an induced coma. The doctor also said that if the swelling did not go down soon, my little angel could die.

The police arrested Mike, but later that night, they came to the hospital and arrested me. Aunt Edna and Uncle Joe stayed at the hospital. Edna said she would call my mother and let her know what was going on. I asked the police why they were arresting me. They said Mike accused me of trying to kill him with a knife. He even went as far as telling the police that I was the one who had caused Michael Jr. to fall against the table and hit his head. I told them that it was all a bunch of lies. They said it was his word against mine, since the only witness was a four-year-old boy who was lying in a hospital bed in a coma.

CHAPTER TWO:

The Beginning

The year was 1981. I grew up on a farm in Loxley, Alabama. There were three of us. My oldest sister Janie was nineteen years old. The youngest, my brother Timmy, was fourteen years old, and I, Sara Ramsey, was sixteen going on thirty. I loved the farm. It was so peaceful and the air was so fresh. On a sunny day, the clouds were white and fluffy. You can always smell honeysuckle in the air.

My mother, Julia, ran the farm. My grandparents died in a plane crash when Janie was a baby. Julia was their only child. They left us a five-bedroom brick house and twenty-seven lovely acres of farmland. We didn't have to worry about the grass. Between the goats and other animals, there wasn't much to cut. Timmy liked to climb the big oak tree off to the side of the house. On a hot day, we'd all take a swim in the lake behind the barn. We had cows, pigs, chickens, horses, and goats. You name it, and we probably had at least one of them. My mama was a hardworking woman who sold milk and eggs to different stores in Loxley. She wasn't rich, but she had enough income to take care of her family and give her farmhands a nice little salary. I admired her for taking care of a huge farm at the age of thirty-six and for being a single parent.

My sister Janie, she was a real firecracker. She didn't take any crap from anybody. The kids at school picked on me a lot.

I wasn't as developed as some of the other girls in my class. They had bigger breasts and looked a lot older than I did. I was tall with long brown hair. My mother always said that my dark-brown eyes were pretty. She often told me that I reminded her of my grandmother. Janie would always come to my rescue no matter what. She'd fight boys, girls, animals, it didn't matter to her. She protected me and Timmy. Janie was pretty, with blonde hair that she liked to keep cut short.

I don't remember my daddy. He left when I was four years old. Mama said she sent him to the store to get some diapers for Timmy and he never came back. Mama never talked bad about him. She just said that he wasn't ready for the responsibility of having a family. She felt maybe they were too young when they got married. Six years later after my dad disappeared, a policeman came out to the farm and told Mama that Daddy had been killed in a car accident in Michigan. Mama was listed as the beneficiary on his life insurance policy. Daddy left us thirty thousand dollars. I'm sad that I never got a chance to know my daddy, but I'm glad he never stopped thinking about his family. I'll always love him for that.

We all had chores to do to help the family business run smoothly. Mama was able to hire a few men to help out with the heavy labor around the farm. One of the guys had a crush on Janie. His name was Rex. The two of them built a nice house on some of the farmland near the stables. I remember one night when we were standing outside under the stars Rex had been drinking with some of the other guys. He and Janie got into a terrible argument. Rex slapped Janie across her face. I prayed that she wouldn't hurt him too bad. Janie grabbed Rex and punched him right in the face. She hit him several times until the other farmhands pulled her off of him. She put a beating on him that night. It didn't matter; the next day they were hugging and kissing like nothing ever happened. One thing I did notice, Rex never got drunk again and tried to hit my sister.

CHAPTER THREE:

The Crush

Time does fly when you're having fun. Two years had gone by already, and I had developed into a young woman. I had the biggest crush on Michael Faraday. Everyone called him Mike. He was also eighteen years old. His father raised and sold horses on his ranch in Loxley. His dad sold my mom a few colts and told her how to start raising horses herself.

Mike was so handsome, tall and muscular, with black hair and a mustache with a little beard. I guess you would call it a goatee. The teachers hated him. They would make him shave, but the hair on his face just kept coming back. Mike was on the football team and drove a 1965 candy-apple-red Mustang. He had a bad boy image. All of the girls in high school liked him. I used to pretend when I was a little girl that I was Barbie and Mike was Ken. I would dress up the two dolls in matching outfits. They were happily married living in their elegant dollhouse. I just knew that one day Mike and I would live happily ever after.

I think Mike's dad had a crush on my mom. He never approached her in that manner, but when he looked at her, it seemed as if he always wanted to say something. Janie said he looked like the devil himself. She said Tom Farraday's eyes were almost black and he looked at you as though he could see right into your soul. He never smiled, and he always smoked a pipe.

There was a sweet, burning smell about him. He mostly let Mike do whatever he wanted to do.

Mrs. Farraday had died while giving birth to Mike. Some people say that Tom Farraday blamed him for her death. Mike was his only child.

Mike was presently dating a girl named Sharon Howser. She was pretty. She reminded me of Farrah Fawcett. She had long, flowing, blonde hair with a huge smile and big beautiful green eyes. They walked around as if they owned the town. Whenever you saw Sharon, Mike wasn't too far behind. The two of them dated for at least two years on and off. We had just started senior year in high school. Then something strange happened. It had to be at least the third or fourth day of school. Sharon stayed at home. Mike was there, but he wasn't his usual self. He hung around with the two guys he normally hangs around with. I spoke to him and he didn't say a word. I noticed he had two long scratches on his left cheek. I asked him what happened. He said he fell off one of the horses at his father's ranch that morning before school.

I had been hearing a lot of whispering going on. I went into the girl's bathroom and overheard some of Sharon's friends saying that she did not come to school because Mike beat her up. I couldn't believe what I was hearing. Impatiently I waited until the end of the school day so I could go to Sharon's house.

Finally, the last school bell rang. I waited for my little brother Timmy. We both walked home together after school. I told him that I had to go to Sharon's house. Timmy didn't want to go with me. He wanted to go home and do his chores around the farm before the sun went down. Curiosity was getting the best of me, though, and I just had to know the truth. Sharon's house stood on the corner of the street. I knocked on the door and her mother answered. She said that Sharon went to visit her aunt and uncle in Saint Louis. I tried to get some information out of Sharon's mother about what happened, but all she said was that Sharon wanted to go and spend some time with her cousins.

Janie saw me and Timmy walking home. "Where have you been?"

"Sara went to Sharon's house to be nosy," Timmy replied.

"I did not; I was just worried when Sharon didn't show up for school today."

"Well, did Mrs. Howser tell you anything, Sara?" Janie asked.

"She told me that Sharon wanted to go and visit with her cousins in Saint Louis."

"Actually, I heard a few stories of my own, little sister. The word around town is that Sharon told Mike that she was pregnant, and she asked him to give her money for an abortion. Mike had been drinking all day, and decided he would beat the crap out of her. The Howsers didn't want the whole town to find out what happened, so they sent her away. Sara, the boy is bad news. Everyone knows that he drinks too much and he will have sex with any girl who's willing or not willing to give it to him. He feels like he can do anything he wants to, and that crazy daddy of his is not going to do a thing about it. Sara, please don't get involved with that guy. He's never going to amount to anything."

I couldn't believe what Janie was saying. I knew it was all some big misunderstanding. Janie kept pleading with me. She was scared that I was about to get into something that I may not be able to get out of. Janie knew that I had a big crush on Mike. I had even refused to go out with any of the other boys in the town, because I always believed in my fantasy world, that Mike and I would eventually get married and live happily ever after. It was all some kind of sick fairy-tale romance. I always believed that there was good in everyone. I didn't realize that some people are just plain evil.

CHAPTER FOUR:

The Relationship Begins

The next morning Mike and his dad brought over a new colt for the stable. His dad looked even stranger than usual. He had that same look in his eyes, but he almost seemed sad. My mom also noticed it and asked him in for a cup of coffee. Usually he refused, saying he was in a hurry to get back to work, but this time he went into the house and had a cup of coffee with my mom. She told Timmy to help Mike with the new colt, but I told Timmy he could go do something else and I'd help Mike.

"Hello. Mike," I said.

"Hello, Sara Ramsey."

"I didn't see your girlfriend at school today. Everyone was talking about her having some sort of accident. Do you know what happened to her?"

"Well, we did have some words. She got angry and scratched the hell out of my face. I got upset about what she did and I slapped her. I didn't mean to hurt her, but when I slapped her, she accidentally fell off the front porch, causing her face and arms to get pretty bruised up. Her family thought it would be best not to make any trouble for anybody, so they sent her to live with her aunt to finish up her senior year."

"I heard that she was pregnant."

"Pregnant! If so, then I'm not the father. Sharon wanted me to spend every minute of the day with her. I've got football practice, and my homework. She didn't want me to hang around any of my friends. I just got sick of her accusing me of having sex with every girl in school. Things just got out of hand. Now…enough about Sharon, let's talk about you and me. Would you like to go horseback riding with me Sara Ramsey?"

I immediately said yes. I was so relieved that he told me the truth about what happened to Sharon. Now I knew what really happened.

Mike and I started spending a lot of time together. Timmy promised that he wouldn't tell Mama or Janie, since they would be angry. I overheard some of the girls at school talking about me and Mike. The jealous ones wanted to know why he was hanging around with an unpopular girl like me. I would pretend not to notice, but a few times I saw him walk up behind some of the cheerleaders and grab their butts.

My friend Liza saw me walking to class.

"Hey, Sara, wait up. We haven't had much time to talk lately."

"I'm sorry Liza; I've just been so busy. With finals coming up and doing my chores at the farm, I don't have a lot of time for anything else."

"You left out one thing, Sara. Mike Farraday. I saw him talking to you the other day and I've heard rumors that he's having sex with you, just like every other girl that he can work his magic charm on."

"Liza, that's not true. Mike likes me, a lot. I love being with him. He makes me feel so special."

Liza swore she had just seen him kissing and fondling some girl in the back of the school parking lot. "Sara, I know what happened to Sharon and the other girls that he beat on in the past."

"Liza, you're just jealous because I have a boyfriend who is handsome and has his own car, and you don't. Boys aren't going to pay any attention to a girl who wears braces and eyeglasses."

I thought about what I said. I saw tears beginning to fall down Liza's face.

"Oh my goodness, I am so sorry. Liza. I didn't mean to say those ugly things to you."

Liza ran down the hallway. We had been friends since second grade. I felt bad for what I had just said to her. I saw Mike walk by with some of the other football players.

"Hello, Mike," I said.

"Not now, Sara! I'll get with you later." They all got into his car and just drove off.

Later that evening, Timmy and I were walking home from school when Mike drove by in his red Mustang.

"Hey, Sara." I kept walking as if I didn't see him. "Sara, I'm sorry that I wasn't able to give you a ride home from school earlier, but I had some important business to take care of."

"You don't even know how to spell business," Timmy replied. Since Mike had apologized to me, I decided to walk over and talk to him. There were several beer cans on the floor of the back seat of the car.

"Why don't you get in, girl, so we can go swimming in the lake?"

"I can't. I've got to study for a biology test and write an essay for English. Besides, I have to make sure Timmy gets home in time, or my mama will get suspicious. I'm already paying him twice a week and doing his homework just to keep him quiet about the two of us. But if you put a smile on your face, Mr. Farraday, I promise to meet you later down by the stables like we planned."

"I don't know, Sara. You know your little brother is beginning to be a real pain in the ass." Mike drove his car up behind me and Timmy real fast as if he was going to hit us. Mike started screaming my name. "Sara, Sara! Get in the car!"

Timmy and I both started running toward the farm.

"No. Not now. I've got to make sure Timmy gets home. I've already wasted too much time talking to you."

Mike kept driving faster and faster. "Stop playing around, Mike!" But he wouldn't; he just started laughing and blowing his car horn . He was beginning to scare me.

Janie was hauling hay down the road to some of the other farmers. She saw Timmy and me running in the middle of the road. Mike stopped his car as soon as he saw Janie's truck. She stopped the truck and got out with a rifle in her hand.

"What in the heck is going on here?"

Mike just kept on laughing. "Hey, Janie, I'm just playing around with Sara and Timmy. I didn't mean any harm."

I also started laughing. "Yeah, Mike was just teasing Timmy and me, that's all." I looked over at Timmy; he had a huge wet spot on the front of his pants. He was so scared that he had urinated on himself. Timmy stood there with tears in his eyes. He ran home as fast as he could. Mike was still laughing as if nothing had happened. Janie picked up the rifle and aimed it at Mike.

"Janie, please," I said. "It was all a big misunderstanding, that's all. It was just a joke. I'm sorry that Timmy got upset."

"Mike Farraday, I don't like you. I've heard that you've got some kind of sick reputation in this town, but if I hear of you trying to do anything to hurt my family, I'll kill you, do you understand?"

Mike stopped laughing and told Janie that he didn't mean any harm. I saw the look in Janie's eyes. It scared me. "Janie, let's just go home, please." I got in the truck. "Please Janie, let's just go. Come on."

"See you later, alligator," Mike replied as he drove away down the street. Janie got in the truck and slammed the door.

"What the hell is he talking about? Sara, have you been seeing that crazy guy? You know, I've been hearing rumors about you and him riding around town together. Ms. Thomas said that she saw you one day out at the Farraday ranch. Have you lost your mind? You know that he beat up Sharon Howser and God knows who else."

"He told me everything that happened. It was Sharon's fault. She started the argument because she was jealous of Mike and some other girls. She scratched his face. Mike was just trying to get her off of him when she accidentally fell off the porch of his house."

"Sara, you are so naive. You'll believe anything that guy tells you. What is it about him that makes you young girls go crazy? He's a liar. Sharon didn't accidentally fall, he beat her up because she was pregnant and he didn't want to pay for the abortion. He took her down by the lake. She asked him for money to get an abortion in the next county and he told her no. He said it wasn't his baby. Sharon kept insisting that he was the only one that she had sex with and that it was his baby and she was going to tell everyone at school that he raped her. That's when your precious Mike Farraday went crazy and beat the poor girl unconscious.

"Some of his so-called football buddies saw everything," Janie continued. "They just left her there lying on the ground. Two old farmers were driving by and heard her screaming for help. They took her to the hospital. They all got together and came up with that stupid story about her falling to keep anyone from finding out that she was pregnant. By the time she got to the hospital, she had lost the baby. Mike gave her an old-fashioned abortion. It's called 'just beat the hell out of her.' Sharon's family didn't want any bad publicity, so they decided to send her away until things got quiet. Liza tried to tell you, but she said that you didn't want to hear the truth."

I sat in the truck not saying a word as we rode home. I didn't want Janie to figure out that I had already had sex with Mike. He had taken me to his house one day while his dad was out of town. He was so soft and gentle. He told me that he loved me and I meant the world to him. It was the happiest day of my life. I just couldn't believe that any of the things being said about Mike were true. I knew that he liked to drink a lot, but he just did it because all the guys on the football team did it. I guess it made them feel important and popular.

CHAPTER FIVE:

I'm Pregnant

About six o'clock that evening, we had just finished dinner. I was so scared that Timmy was going to tell my mom what had happened earlier that day. He was quiet. Mama asked him if he was feeling alright. He just told her he was going to bed early because he was tired. I didn't feel so well myself. I felt nauseated and tired. I figured it was because of all the stress that had been going on lately and trying to keep me dating Mike a secret. It was getting to be a little too much to handle. I missed talking to my best friend, Liza. We used to be so close.

I went to bed that night, but when I woke up the next day, I was sicker than I had ever been in my life. I was dizzy, tired, and weak. I couldn't go to school that morning. I couldn't even get out of bed.

"Sara, what's going on, sweetie?" Mama asked. "That's not like you to miss a day of school."

Janie was standing in my bedroom doorway next to Mama. She mumbled under her breath, "She's probably got a bun in the oven."

"What did you say, Janie?"

"I didn't say anything, Mama. You know me, I was just joking around. I'm just kidding, you guys."

"Are you a virgin, Sara?" Mama asked.

"Mama...I'm sure it's just the flu or maybe a stomach virus."

"I asked you if you were a virgin, Sara. Now you answer me!"

I saw a look in my mom's eyes that I had never seen before. I was scared. Janie was standing there looking at me also. I felt the tears rolling down my face. Truth, please set me free.

"No, Mama. I'm not a virgin. I've been having sex with Mike."

Mama grabbed my arms. "Did the two of you use protection?"

"Mike said he did."

She just kept shaking me. "Did you see him put on a condom? Sara Ramsey, did you see him put on a damn condom?"

The tears just kept rolling down my face. I was so terrified. "No, Mama. I didn't see him put one on, but he said he used one each time we made love."

Mama was devastated. She started screaming as if someone had stabbed her in the back with a knife. "Get up out of that bed and get dressed," Mama said as she stormed out of my bedroom.

Janie drove us down to the local clinic. I sat there for at least three hours. I felt like the inside of my body was turned upside down. They finally called me into the exam room. The nurse took my blood and a urine specimen. She came back twenty minutes later and told me that I was definitely pregnant. Janie told me to have an abortion, but I didn't want to. I loved Mike and I wanted to have his baby. Mama didn't say much. She was upset and disappointed with me.

The doctor examined me and said that there was an abnormality with my uterus and it was a possibility that I may not be able to carry the baby full term. She gave me some prenatal vitamins and suggested I get as much rest as possible. She also recommended some exercises that would make my uterus stronger.

It was a long and quiet ride back to the farm. I tried to explain to Mama that everything would be just fine. I would graduate from high school in the summer, and the baby would be born in the fall. We could live on the farm until the baby got older; then I could go to college and get my degree in business or agriculture. I was sure Mike would want to help out as well. Who knows, maybe we could even get married.

"I think everything will be alright, Mama."

"You have made a big mistake," Mama replied.

"Sara, I'll help you as much as I can because I love you and maybe somehow all of this is my fault. I know your dad wasn't around, and I didn't try to marry or get involved with anyone else after he died. Maybe I'm the one to blame." Mama got out of the truck and walked into the house.

CHAPTER SIX:

Mike's Reaction

A few days later, I went back to school. Some of the kids were whispering about Mike and me. Mike didn't come to school that day. Liza came up to me and said she heard that I was pregnant.

"Yeah, it's true. I am pregnant, but please don't tell anyone."

"It's a little too late for that, Sara. All of the kids here are talking about it. How do you think I found out? Are you going to get an abortion?"

"Liza, I wasn't planning on having an abortion. I want my baby."

We sat down at one of the tables next to the cafeteria. Liza looked at me as if she wanted to cry. We ate lunch together. I was so glad I had Liza to talk to again.

"I am sorry for all of those ugly things that I said the other day, Liza. You know that you're my best friend and I didn't mean any of those things."

"Well, Sara, I'm sorry for you. You're going to need a good friend now more than ever."

I saw Mike later that evening down by the lake.

"Hey, Sara, what took you so long?"

"Mike, we need to talk."

"Talk? I don't want to talk, Sara. Trust me, there are too many other things that we can be doing. Why don't you come and lie next to me on this blanket and I'll show you."

I stood there next to an oak tree.

"Mike, I'm pregnant."

He just lay there laughing. "Sara, why are you joking? I'm not in the mood for any school girl jokes right now."

"I'm serious. I am pregnant. I found out a few days ago. It's your baby."

Mike stood up and walked over to me. "Have you made an appointment for an abortion?"

"No. I wasn't planning on having an abortion. The baby is not due until after I graduate. I thought once the baby is born, then maybe we can get married or get a little place of our own. Your dad pays you for working on the ranch, and Mama pays me for working on the farm."

But before I could even finish what I was saying, I noticed Mike's face was turning red. He got so angry that he grabbed my neck with both of his hands and started to choke me.

"You are going to get an abortion. Do you hear me, Sara? You are not going to destroy my life." He just kept yelling and screaming that I get an abortion now. I could smell the alcohol on his breath. My feet kept sliding around in the mud by the lake.

I accidentally fell down on the ground when Mike started choking me. He grabbed my head and shoved it under the water. I kept trying to fight to get up. I couldn't believe this was happening. He finally pulled me up by my hair. I felt myself slowly losing conscious. Coughing, grasping for air. Water streamed from my mouth and nose as my body lay helplessly on the ground.

"Sara. Sara. I am so sorry. Baby I didn't mean to hurt you. Are you alright? Speak to me. Just say something. Sara, I'm under a lot of pressure. People talking about what happened to Sharon. My dad hates me. I'm about to lose my mind, Sara.

Now you're telling me that you're pregnant. Hell, I just don't think I can handle much more."

He started crying. I felt so sorry for him. Mike helped me up and we started to hug each other."Please just tell me you're alright."

I nodded my head, letting Mike know that I was feeling better.

"I've got to get you dried off, Sara. Come over here, I've got some towels in my car. Sara, you know that I love you and I would never hurt you, right? Promise me that you won't tell anyone what happened here today."

"Mike, I love you too. I know that you've got a lot going on right now. I didn't mean to make matters worse for you. We won't talk about what happened today ever again."

CHAPTER SEVEN:

Baby Drama

One day I woke up with the worst pain in my back and stomach. I thought I was going to die. Janie and Mama drove me to the hospital. The doctor said that my blood pressure was high and my blood sugar level was elevated. The doctor told my mama that if I didn't quit school and start bed rest immediately, I could go into premature labor. Both the baby and I could die. The only solution to the problem was for me to quit school and stay in bed resting until the baby was born. I only had three more months left in school.

The test also showed that my uterus was just too weak to carry the baby full term if I was up and about on my feet all the time. Man, was I upset. I wanted to graduate with Mike and the rest of my class, but I also wanted to have a healthy baby.

"Don't worry Sara," Janie replied. "You can always get your GED after the baby is born."

I went home later that day from the hospital. Mama talked with the principal at my high school. They were nice about everything. I don't think they wanted pregnant girls attending their school. There were only three pregnant girls that I knew of that attended Loxley High, and I was the third one. They were strict about teenagers having sex. They told Mama that as soon as I was ready, they would arrange for me to take my GED exam.

I stayed at home in bed with my feet elevated. Liza came by to see me every day after school. She tried to help me with school assignments and homework, just so I wouldn't get too far behind. I had decided to go along with the school's recommendations and just let them know when I was ready to take my GED exam.

The time went by so fast. Soon graduation was just two weeks away. My stomach was big. I felt so uncomfortable. I wanted this baby, but I didn't know all the hell I would have to go through just to have it. I was seven months pregnant. How I hated looking at myself in the mirror. My skin was red and dry. People told me that my feet were swollen; I hadn't been able to see them in the last few weeks because of my big stomach. My back hurts all the time. Mama had to buy me a bedside commode to use because I could no longer get to the bathroom in time. I wasn't sure if I was doing the right thing or not. Maybe I should have had an abortion like everyone suggested. I wanted to cry sometimes. But when I looked at my ultrasound picture, it made me feel so much better, just to know that I had a beautiful little girl growing inside of me. It made all of the suffering worthwhile. I loved my baby. I was going to name her Michelle. She would be named after the two most important people in my life, Mike and my mama, Julia Michelle.

I had only seen Mike a few times. Mama finally agreed to let him come to the house to see me. He would only visit for about ten minutes.

"Hi, Mike. I'm glad that you came by to visit today. I really wish I could go to the graduation, but I'm still on bed rest. Have you made any plans?"

"No, not really. A friend of mine offered me a job, but I'll have to wait a few years before I can take it."

"Someone offered you a job here in Loxley?"

"No, Sara. This job is in Florida."

"You know people in Florida?"

"Yes. I have relatives and friends there. That's what I'm planning on doing in a few years. From what I was told, the money is easy to make."

"What about our baby?"

"Well, you said that you were going to stay here on the farm with your family. They can help you raise her, and of course you know that I will send you money and come down to see you. Who knows, maybe we can get married one day."

"What about after graduation, Mike? What are you going to do then?"

"I guess I'll just continue to work for my dad until I find a job in Florida that I can do for a couple of years. That will give me time to find a place to stay. Sara, all I can do is take it one day at a time. I was depending on that football scholarship, but since it fell through, I'm just gonna have to take it slow. Look, I've got to get out of here. I'll talk to you later. Take care of yourself. See you soon." Mike kissed me on the forehead and left. He never answered any of my questions. Where do Michelle and I fit in his life?

My friend Liza came by the house to see me. She was so excited about graduation coming up next week.

"Sara, I hate to be the one to deliver bad news, but I saw Mike hanging around with one of the new cheerleaders."

"Mike told me that he only hangs around with the cheerleaders because that's what football players do. It's expected of them to date cheerleaders. He's not interested in her. He wasn't interested in Sharon Howser either."

"I'm not sure about that, Sara. He and Sharon had been dating on and off since middle school. I think he really did like her, in his own strange way. He just didn't want to get any more money from his dad for an abortion again."

"What do you mean, an abortion again? Liza, those stories aren't true. Mike said that he never got Sharon pregnant."

"Well, one thing we do know for certain, Miss Sara Ramsey, he got you pregnant."

"Mike Farraday loves me and he said as soon as our little girl is born, we're gonna get married."

"Sara, did Mike actually say he was going to marry you?"

"Well...not in so many words, but I know once the baby arrives, he'll calm down and see things differently. Liza, I have loved Mike Farraday the majority of my life. Even when I was a little girl. That's why we made love that day. He picked me up from school and we went to his house when his dad was out of town. He told me that I was always the one that he loved. He had to hang around with those girls, because the other football players made him. They would have called him names if he didn't go out with the cheerleaders. Liza, he told me that he had sex with some of those girls, but it didn't mean anything and he always wore a condom. Mike knew from the first day he saw me at the farm that we had a future together. You see, Liza? He feels the same way that I do. Why can't you just wish the best for us?"

"Sara, I want to, but the guy is crazy. He's a drunk and when he drinks he's out of control. There's nothing you can do about that, Sara. He's going to end up hurting someone or even killing someone. You've got your family and your friends. It's not too late for you. Just let go and let Mike walk away."

Liza held my hand as she had tears in her eyes.

"I'm going to forgive you for saying all those things, Liza," I said. "I know you've never been in love, so you don't know how it feels." I just lay there staring at the wall until Liza went home.

CHAPTER EIGHT:

The Birth of Michelle

Three weeks had gone by. Everyone in senior class was running around deciding what college to attend or what to do now that graduation was over. I was a little jealous because everyone graduated and I couldn't. I felt better, because I knew as soon as the baby arrived, everything would get back to normal. I hadn't heard from or seen Mike since graduation. His father would come by to see my mom, but Mike didn't come with him anymore.

One morning I felt a wet spot in my bed. My stomach and back had been bothering me during the night.

"Sara, you've got to go to the hospital now," Mama said. "Your water just broke. I'm going to call an ambulance to take you to the hospital."

When I got there, my blood pressure was still high and the baby was in distress. The doctor had to perform a C-section. I had to be put to sleep for my blood pressure to start going down. When I woke up that evening, Mama and Janie were in the room with me. They said that Timmy was at the nursery looking at the baby.

"How does she look, Mama?"

"She is as cute as a button, Sara. She weighs seven pounds. She looks just like you when you were a baby."

"No, Mama," Janie said. "Actually, she looks just like Mike Farraday."

"I don't care who she looks like, I just can't wait to hold my baby girl in my arms."

"I'll walk down to the nursery and see if they can bring her to your room," Janie said.

"Thank you, Janie."

Tom came to the hospital. I was shocked to see him. Mike came with him. I was so happy, I started to cry. Regardless of what Mike said, I knew that he loved his baby just as much as I did.

"Hello, Sara."

"Hi, Mr. Farraday. Hi, Mike."

"Hey, Sara."

"That sure is a beautiful little granddaughter that you two youngsters produced. She looks a little bit like her granddaddy over here."

"Now, Tom Farraday, I was thinking she looks a little bit like her grandmother over here." Both Mama and Tom started laughing.

Mike was quiet. He just stood in the corner keeping all comments to himself. We all heard a knock on the door.

"Come in," I replied. "Oh...There's my little angel." The nurse brought the baby into the room, along with some papers. Timmy and Janie came into the room also.

"Mike, would you like to hold your daughter Michelle?"

"No...I don't feel real comfortable right now. Maybe you can show me how to hold her later."

"Alright."

"I think she's hungry, Ms. Ramsey," the nurse said. "I bought you a couple of bottles for her. She really likes to eat."

"I'll feed her."

"Ms. Ramsey, I have the baby's birth certificate here. It needs to be signed by the father."

"Mama and Timmy, why don't we go downstairs for some lunch," Janie said. "I'm getting hungry."

"Sounds like a good idea," Mama said. "Sara, we'll be back in a little while. Tom, would you like to join us?"

"No. I want to talk to Mike and Sara for a little while."

"We love you Sara and Michelle. She is so adorable. We'll be back later."

Tom had a serious look on his face.

"Mike, son, come over here and stand next to your family. I want you to sign this birth certificate in order to claim that beautiful little girl. Hell, she looks just like you anyway." We all started laughing.

"This is your responsibility," he continued. "Your life will never be the same. You are a man now. It's time that you step up to the plate. Sara, Mike and I have been doing some talking. Mike's grandfather died about few years ago. He left his house and property to me. The house is located in a small city in Florida called Henderson. It's only about one hundred miles from Loxley. Mike and I looked at the house a few days ago. It doesn't need much work done to it. While you and the baby are getting stronger at the farm, Mike and some of the ranch hands can get started renovating the house. It's a three-bedroom house, with a nice size family room and kitchen. It's perfect for the three of you. My sister Edna and her husband Joe also live in that town. Mike's uncle Joe said he's sure that he can get him a job at the local coal mine. Edna owns a dress shop. Sara, she said she'd be willing to give you a job. I know it's a pretty big pill to swallow right now, and if you want to think about it, I understand."

"No. No. I don't have to think about it, Mr. Farraday. It sounds like a great idea. Just perfect."

"Well, first of all, Sara, if we are going to be family, you've got to stop calling me Mr. Farraday and call me Tom."

"Alright, Tom. I can do that."

"I also think that the two of you should get married first. That way the baby will have her truth birthright name." Mike still didn't say anything. He just signed the birth certificate and let Tom did all the talking. Tears of joy rolled down my face. Everything that I had ever wished for was about to come true.

We stayed in the hospital for five days. I still felt a little sore, but the baby was getting stronger every day. I loved the way she smelled. Like a new spring day. Her skin was so soft and precious. She had a headof black hair and her eyes were big and brown. She was definitely Michael Farraday's baby girl.

Immediately after I was released from the hospital, Mike and I were married at the courthouse. About a month went by. I attended the night classes at my high school and received my GED. Michelle was growing so fast. Mama loved that baby. Janie continued to try to convince me not to leave with Mike. She said the baby and I could keep living at the farm. Rex and the other farmhands even offered to build me a house next to Mama's, but I told them no.They were so afraid that if I left the farm, they would never see me and Michelle again. I told them it was only one hundred miles to Henderson.They could drive up or we could drive down anytime we wanted to visit. I told Mama I couldn't let Mike down. He was working so hard to fix up the house for his family. He was trying very hard. I couldn't let him down.

It took three months before the house was finished. I had been packing up my things and the baby's belongings. We were both ready to leave the farm and go to our new home. Liza came by the farm to visit Michelle and me.

"Hey, Sara. I've missed you so much. Look at Michelle. She looks just like a little angel. Oh…Look at that smile. Can I please hold her?"

"Yes, you can hold her. I thought you'd be headed off to school somewhere."

"Give me a break. I just went to school for twelve years. Forgive me if I'm just a little tired and I want to take a small break."

"I guess I can forgive you this time, madam."

"Sara, I didn't just come here to help you pack your things. I heard some bad stuff about Mike. I know that you are going to get mad and probably hate me for telling you, but I am your friend and I do give a damn about you. I just want you to be sure that you know what you are walking into."

"What is it this time? Let me guess, he's been kissing cheerleaders in the parking lot again. Liza, we have had this conversation a hundred times. Mike hasn't done anything. He's been in Florida the past few months working on our house. There are several guys who can witness to his whereabouts."

"The real reason that Mike had to marry you is because a thirteen-year-old girl said that he raped her. The girl's family told Tom that he better get Mike out of town before they kill him. This happened about four months ago. Yeah...just before Michelle was born. That's why Tom came up with this brilliant idea that the two of you get married and get the hell out of Loxley."

"That can't be true. Tom would have told my mom. That girl's family would have called the police if that was true."

"She admitted to her family later that night that she consented to having sex with Mike. She knew how old he was and he knew how old she was. The girl's father used to work for Tom at the ranch. That's why no one called the police. Did you just here what I said? The man had sex with a thirteen-year-old girl."

"I heard what you said. That's just a bunch of gossip. Did you talk to this so-called little girl?"

"No, but—"

"No, Liza. I don't want to talk about this anymore! You've been bad-mouthing Mike for years now and I'm sick and tired of it. Please just help me pack. We have to leave soon."

Liza stood there looking at me. Her stare was so intense; I could feel the heat from her eyes. She didn't mention anything else about Mike. After we finished packing, Liza hugged me and gave Michelle a big kiss. With tears in her eyes, she stated, "Sara, I love you. If you need me ever for anything, you know where to find me."

Janie and Mama drove me and the baby to the new house. I was so excited, but I was also sad. I was going to miss that farm.

Mama didn't say much during the drive. Janie kept reminding me if I need anything to just call, and it's OK if I want to come back home. When we finally got to the house, Mike and his dad were already there. It was a big white house trimmed in baby blue with a swing on the front porch. A white picket fence surrounded the house. It was like something out of a fairy tale. The yard was big. They had done a great job renovating the house. Everyone helped unload the truck.

We got settled in pretty fast. The house was filled with beautiful antique furniture. Mike even bought an old baby bed at a yard sale and polished it up for the baby. He was working five days a week at the coal mine with his uncle Joe. I started my new job with Aunt Edna at the dress shop. I found a nice church daycare to take Michelle to. It was hard working at the dress shop. I was so used to working on the farm, but it didn't take me long to adjust to selling clothes. Edna also taught me how to sew and knit, since the majority of her products were handmade. Aunt Edna was so nice to me. She showed me how to run a shop. I had been attending a business vocational program in the evenings and on my lunch break. Mike would watch Michelle in the evenings when he got off work until I got home. Everything was going pretty well the first year. I started taking some accounting courses. I had even made enough money to get myself a used car. It wasn't anything fancy, but it had a great engine. Mama called every day to check on me and Michelle. Mike kept saying if Mama didn't stop calling that house so much, he would rip the phone out of the wall. I told Mama that she didn't have to call every day. I didn't tell her that Mike had threatened to destroy the phone if she kept calling so much.

CHAPTER NINE:

And So It Begins

I got home from school one night around seven as usual. I heard Michelle screaming and crying when I got out of my car. Immediately, I ran to the front door and opened it. Michelle was standing at the door. Her diaper was soak with urine and soiled with feces. Her face was so red. I picked her up and took her into the bedroom. Mike was sitting in the living room in his recliner chair. He was totally knocked out. I took Michelle into the bathroom and gave her a nice warm bath.

"Come on, sweetie. Mama's gonna put you in your favorite pajamas. Yes, I am. Are you hungry? Is Mommy's little angel hungry? There...Now you look so pretty."

I glanced over at Mike as Michelle and I went into the kitchen. He had at least twelve beer cans lying on the floor next to his chair. He couldn't have heard a bomb if it had exploded in his face.

"Mommy's got your favorite, Michelle, macaroni and cheese. Do you want some milk? How about some chocolate milk for my special girl." She was so happy. My poor baby was so hungry.

After Michelle ate her supper, she immediately fell asleep in my arms. I carried her into the bedroom and laid her in the baby bed. I cleaned up the kitchen, took a shower, and proceeded to get ready for bed myself. Mike finally woke up. He walked into the bedroom.

"It's about time you got home to shut that kid up."

"What did you just say, Mike?" Mad and highly disappointed, I walked up to him and slapped him across his face. "How could you get drunk and fall asleep? You should have been watching Michelle. I heard her crying when I drove up in the driveway. She was soaked and had dried feces on her bottom. Did you even change her diaper? Did you even feed her? What did you do when you got off work? From the looks of things, it seems if though you just sat in that recliner chair of yours and drank two six-packs. How could you be so irresponsible? What if Michelle had wandered outside into the street? Anything could have happened while you were sitting over there asleep!"

Mike walked up to me and slapped me across my face. He hit me so hard that I fell down to the floor. A drop of blood flew out of my mouth. He grabbed me by my hair. I went down to my knees from the pain. He dragged me across the bedroom floor and slammed the door. He then proceeded to kick me in the stomach and punch me in the back.

"Mike, please stop! You're hurting me, please stop!" He finally stopped. If he hadn't been so drunk, I think he would have killed me.

"If you ever put your hands on me again, Sara, I'll kill you. I'm Mike Farraday. I'm the man of this house. You need to stay at home and take care of that brat. Hell, she's probably not my kid anyway. All of those farmhands your mama had working for her, she might belong to one of them."

I just lay on the floor, too scared to move. He sat on the bed and started crying.

"It's all your fault. Girls like you and Sharon Howser are always making things hard for a man. I didn't want to get married. My dad told me I had to marry you and leave Loxley. Some crazy kid told her folks that I had sex with her. I didn't know she was thirteen. She looked like a grown woman to me, plus it only happened one time. My friends from high school are out going to college and having a good time. I'm stuck here in Henderson working in a coal mine. I hate this place. Uncle Joe bosses me around all day. Do this, Mike, do that, Mike, and then I come home to you and that screaming kid. I don't like hitting women. You made me do it, Sara. I'm going into the living room so I can get some sleep. You stay in this room, Sara. I don't want to see your face anymore tonight."

Mike walked out of the room and shut the door. I continued to lie on the floor, thinking, is this a dream? What just happened to me? I'd heard so many different stories about Mike beating up girls, but I never thought he would do this to me.

I managed to get myself up off the floor. Was I paralyzed? No. I was able to walk—barely. Tears were rolling down my face. I was in so much pain. I didn't think anything was broken. I was just very sore. I lay across the bed for a while until I heard him snoring. I snuck into Michelle's room. I picked her up and carried her into my bedroom with me. We both lay in bed. I tossed and turned half the night, trying desperately to get comfortable. So shocked by everything that had taken place, I don't think I slept at all that night.

The next morning, Mike came into the bedroom.

"Sara. Hey, baby. Don't be afraid. I am sorry about last night. I had been drinking too much and I wasn't thinking straight. Baby, I'll never do anything to hurt you again. Michelle, baby girl, Daddy is so sorry for not taking better care of you."

He noticed the bruise I had on my left cheek. "Sara, why don't you stay at home from work today and get some rest? I'll tell Aunt Edna that you've got some kind of virus and you don't feel well. As a matter of fact, why don't you just stay in the house today and if anybody calls, don't answer the phone. I promise I won't hit you again. I love you, Sara."

Mike kissed me and Michelle before he went to work. As soon as Mike left, I got up and struggled to the medicine cabinet. My body was hurting so bad. I wondered if my ribs were broken. I decided to just take something for pain and lay back down for a while with Michelle.

Later that day, Mike came home from work, bringing a dozen long-stemmed red roses and three steak dinners. "Hey, sweetheart. I thought about you all day."

Mike kissed me. His lips were dry and he smelled like coal dust. "How are you feeling?"

"I'm still in a lot of pain, Mike."

"Well, you'll feel much better soon. Look, I got you some roses. I know how much you love red roses, and since you couldn't go out, I brought dinner to you."

"I fried chicken for dinner."

"That's alright. We'll just eat it tomorrow. I want to celebrate tonight with my favorite girls."

We watched the football game after we ate dinner. Mike cleaned up the kitchen while I gave Michelle her bath and put her to bed. Mike and I went into our bedroom. He wanted to have sex. I didn't want to because I was still pretty sore from last night, but I was afraid if I said no, he would beat me again.

"Come on, Sara, I'll be gentle with you. I know that you're still hurt. I promise that it won't happen again. Just let me make love to you." He kissed me gently on the forehead and then on my lips. I just smiled and lay on the bed as my body endured the pain in order for him to receive the pleasure.

I went back to work the next day after dropping Michelle off at the daycare. I still had a visible bruise on my left cheek. I tried to put on enough makeup that no one could see it, but Edna still noticed my face.

"Good morning, Sara. You know, Joe woke up with some kind of stomach virus this morning too. Sara, what happened to your face? Is something wrong with your cheek? It almost looks bruised."

"Yeah, I tripped over one of Michelle's toys. No matter how many times I tell her to pick up her things, she still leaves something lying on the floor. Edna, I've been thinking. I'm not gonna take any business courses next semester."

"Why? You are so close to finishing the program."

"I know. It's just that Michelle is growing up so fast. She's already two years old. I want to spend more time at home doing things with my baby girl. These moments are so precious in a child's life. When she gets a little older, then I'll finish the rest of my courses."

"Sara, do you need anything? Look, you're married to my nephew. Trust me, I know him well. If you or Michelle need anything, don't ever hesitate to ask me or Joe."

"No. I just need to be at home right now."

"I understand. Oh, Sara, your face looks just fine. No one will notice the bruise." Edna walked off and left me standing there wondering. Was she aware of the beating that I had suffered at the hands of Mike?

CHAPTER TEN:

Happy Birthday

Everything seemed to be alright for about a year. On Mike's birthday that year, he turned twenty-one. Edna agreed to watch Michelle for the night. I made plans to take Mike out for a romantic dinner and then later for dancing. Mike loved country and western music. The bedroom was filled with rose petals and scented candles. This was going to be a special night for the both of us.

When Mike got home that evening from work, he had an even bigger surprise in store for me.

"Hey, Mike. Happy birthday to you. I have got the perfect present planned for you tonight, baby."

"I've got a present for you too, Sara. I quit my job."

"You quit your job? Why did you do that?"

"Because I hate that damn coal mine. I am twenty-one years old today. I don't have to do what Uncle Joe or my daddy says anymore. I am a grown man. Finally! I can do what the hell I want to do."

I could smell the liquor on his breath.

"I'm going out to party with the boys tonight," Mike said.

"Sweetie, I was planning on taking you out to dinner and dancing tonight. Everything is already planned. Michelle is with Edna for the rest of the evening. Honey, we've got the house to ourselves. It's been almost three years since we've had the house to ourselves."

"Well, Sara, I've already made plans too. These guys offered me a job at one of the hottest clubs in Florida. Girl, I've got a chance to really make some money. I can't let them down. I told them I'd come by and check out their club tonight."

"Mike, can you please change your plans just this one time?"

Mike's eyes became red as fire. Sweat was dripping off his forehead. The taste of fear filled my mouth. Mike punched me in the stomach with his fist. He hit me so hard that I couldn't breathe. It knocked the wind out of my body, and I went down to the floor on my knees.

"Sara, I told you I was going out tonight and I mean it!"

He pushed me over onto the floor and just walked out of the house.

Later that evening, I swept up the rose petals and put away the scented candles that I had prepared in the bedroom. I sat around thinking maybe he would just go out with the guys for a little while and then he would come back home. I lay across the bed, but Mike never came back home that night. When I woke up the next morning, I decided since it was the weekend, I'd take Michelle down to the farm to visit with Mama. She had only visited the farm once, but she adored the animals. Mike was still nowhere in sight. I packed some of Michelle's things and called out to the farm. Janie answered the phone.

"Sara Ann Ramsey, is that you, girl?"

"Janie, my name is Sara Ann Farraday, ma'am."

"Well, you will always be Sara Ann Ramsey to me, little sister. So, how are you doing?

"I'm alright."

"Really? You don't sound alright. Actually, you don't sound alright at all.

What has your wonderful husband Mike Farraday done this time?"

"Nothing. Michelle wanted to come by and see the animals, so I thought we would drive out for a visit today. If it's alright with Mama?"

"You know that it's alright with Mama. Come on out here. I know the two of you are gonna spend the night?"

"Yes. I had planned on us spending the night."

"Good. I'll get your old room ready for you and Michelle. Sara, are you sure you're alright? I don't mind coming to Henderson to kick Mike's butt if there is a problem."

"Janie, are you ever going to change?"

"No. Now get off this phone, Sara Ann Ramsey, and bring my niece here so I can see her. I love you, Sara. Be careful. See you when you get here. Bye."

"Bye, Janie."

I wasn't sure when Mike will be back, so I left him a note letting him know that Michelle and I had gone to Loxley for the weekend to visit.

Everyone was so happy to see us when we arrived. I must admit, I hadn't felt that comfortable and safe since I left the farm. Janie and Rex were talking about getting married. I was happy to hear that. Mama was still dating Mr. Farraday. I didn't think they would ever get married, but I was glad that they were there for each other. Timmy was so tall. He was a freshman at the local college, majoring in chemical engineering. He was also dating a lovely young lady.

Michelle spent most of the day playing with the animals on the farm. Rex and Janie took her riding on one of the ponies. I drove downtown and ran into an old friend of mine at the store. It was Liza. She had changed. Wow, what a difference three years can make. She was tall and thin with long blonde hair. Instead of eyeglasses, she wore contact lenses, a clear blue color that reminded me of the ocean. She had her braces removed and her teeth looked spectacular. I hardly recognized her. We talked for a while. She said she was teaching second grade at Loxley Elementary. She had two more years of college left, and then she would have her master's degree and become a professor at the local university. She had her life together. I told her I would soon have my master's in business and accounting. I told her that Mike and I were doing so well. I told so many lies that day, if I were Pinocchio, my nose would have grown at least ten miles long.

I enjoyed seeing Mama. I wanted to hug her so tight and never let her go. I missed her strength and courage. I felt so weak and stupid. Mike is probably right, I thought; all of this is my fault.

When the weekend was over, it was time to drive back home. Part of me wanted to go home, but a part of me deep inside wanted to go back to my old room and just stay there. Mama looked at me and just said, "If you need me for anything, I'm right here. Don't you ever forget it."

We drove back to the house. Mike's car was still gone. I got Michelle in and ready for bed. She was so tired. The note that I left for him was still stuck to the refrigerator door. I wasn't sure if he had come home or not. I did some cleaning around the house, then I went to bed. I did not know if I should call the police and report him missing or just wait for him to come home. He wouldn't buy a beeper or a cell phone like I asked him to. Mike said that those things were only used by women to keep up with men and their every move. I finally fell asleep across the bed.

Mike came home that morning driving a brand new candy-apple-red convertible Mustang. I was up getting ready for work that Monday morning.

"Hello, Mike." I kissed him softly on his lips.

"Good morning, Sara baby." I was afraid to ask him where he had been all weekend. I did somehow bring up enough nerve to ask him about the car. "Mike, sweetie, I love that car."

"Well, I got that job that I was telling you about at Big Billy's Lounge. I can finally afford to live a little. This job pays more than working in a coal mine. I don't have to answer to anyone because I am my own boss."

"That sounds like a pretty good job." Constantly keeping a sexy little smile on my face, I asked him, "Where is this place located, sweetie?"

"Just on the outskirts of Henderson. The location is great. A lot of guys come through while traveling. They're starting me off as a bouncer and a bartender, but in a year or so, if I play my cards right, I can move up to assistant manager. I'll be working the night shift, so I don't want to hear you complaining about me being out all night long, do you understand? This is my big opportunity to make some money. I tell you, Sara, this place is gonna be a gold mine. I've been telling Billy that for years."

"Who is Billy?"

"Big Billy Harris. I've known him since I was a little boy. We used to play together when I came down to visit my granddaddy here in Henderson. I taught that fool how to ride a horse. I even told him how to make out with girls. Billy was like the brother I never had."

"You never mentioned him before when we arrived here to Henderson."

"What?"

"I said you never mentioned his name before. Maybe you could have invited him over for dinner some night, and you could have introduced him to your family."

"Whatever, Sara. Look, it's getting late. It's time for you to go to work. Can't have Aunt Edna docking your pay. Go on, girl, get out of here."

"Alright, sweetheart. I left you some breakfast on the stove. I'll see you later." As I kissed him goodbye, he smelled of a combination of stale beer and an old chimney. I didn't know what to think. I was afraid to tell him that I felt like he was making a big mistake quitting his job at the coal mine.

I got Michelle and took her out to the car. She was a little cranky this morning. Probably from too much excitement this weekend at the farm.

Michelle and I finally made it to the daycare center. Monday morning traffic was a headache. I proceeded on to work, driving like a madwoman. Didn't want to be late for my first day as assistant manager. I got a pay raise also, but I didn't want to discuss that with Mike just yet. Good, no one was standing in the parking lot as I drove up. I quickly ran in the back door of the store. No one noticed that I was running a few minutes late.

"Good morning, Sara. How was your weekend?" Wow, talk about good timing. I made it into my office and sat down at the desk just as Edna walked by the door.

"Good morning, Aunt Edna. Michelle and I had a great time at the farm. It's so beautiful there. Azaleas are blooming everywhere. Everyone was so happy to see the both of us. I didn't realize how much I miss my family."

"Joe had a big falling out with Mike about quitting his job at the coal mine," Edna said. "You know he's working at some strip club on the outskirts of town. He's acting like a real pimp. Sara, Joe and I aren't blind. If you need anything, please tell us. Mike is my nephew and I love him, but I know that he's not the world's best husband. He'll break your heart, Sara. Please be careful."

"Mike did tell me that he was working at some lounge on the outskirts of town, but he said that he was a bouncer and a bartender. I don't know anything about a pimp."

"Well, Joe has heard several different rumors about Big Billy's Lounge from the guys who work at the coal mine. They say all kinds of things go on in that place. Women stripping and having sex with men. I've even heard stories about men having sex with men, but like I said, I don't know. Just be careful, that's all I'm saying, and if you need anything either for yourself or for Michelle, please don't hesitate to ask."

I gave Edna a big hug and went on with my usual work schedule. We didn't speak about Mike anymore that day.

Mike continued to keep coming home every morning smelling like liquor and cheap women's perfume. Sometimes he would come home at four or five in the morning wanting to have sex.

"Sara...Hey, Sara."

"Mike. Is that you? It's four o'clock in the morning, baby. Why aren't you at work?"

"Baby, I missed you so bad. I just had to come home and touch you." Oh, he smelled so bad.

"Did you save some liquor for your customers or did you drink it all?"

"Come on, Sara... That's not funny." He continued to laugh as he put one hand on my breast and the other hand under my gown.

"Mike, baby, please. I've got to get up in a couple of hours and get dressed for work. Please, not right now. Later, baby. I promise. I'm so sleepy. No, honey!"

Mike straddled my body and put his hands around my neck. He kept trying to kiss me, but the hair on his face where he so desperately needed a shave was literally cutting my skin.

"You listen to me, bitch. If you don't do what I tell you to do, I'll kill you. Do you understand me?"

"Yes... yes, Mike. I'll do whatever you want me to do."

"Turn over on your stomach. I don't even want to look at your face." I rolled over onto my stomach, just like Mike told me to. He pushed my gown up toward my neck and began to kiss me on my back. I could feel him jamming his penis inside of me. He forced me to have anal sex. I put my hands over my mouth to keep from screaming. The pain was almost unbearable. I was glad that he had been drinking. After the first minute, he fell over onto the bed and passed out. I just lay there, too afraid to move.

The next day he came home about four thirty that morning. I was awakened again to the smells of stale beer and cheap women's perfume. He made me give him oral sex. Too afraid to say anything, I simply got up and went down on my hands and knees on the floor. Mike pulled down his pants and sat on the edge of the bed. I noticed he had lipstick on his penis. I see some other woman had already been there before me. Tears rolled down my face.

Afterward, I took a long hot shower. My body felt so dirty. I knew somehow that all of this was my fault. Maybe if I could just be a better wife, he wouldn't feel as if he had to go out and be with other woman. I heard a loud knock on the shower door. It was Mike.

"Get out here and make me some breakfast, and you better not use up all of the hot water." I immediately came out of the shower. I got dressed quickly and headed toward the kitchen. Michelle was still asleep. I moved around quietly. I didn't want to wake her up.

I got some bacon and a carton of eggs out of the refrigerator. Mike had just finished his shower as I was putting his plate on the table. I scrambled him three eggs, fried four slices of bacon, chopped up three fresh strawberries, and gave him two slices of toast. All of his favorites. He walked into the kitchen wearing a pair of flannel pajamas as if it were freezing in the house. Mike placed a bottle of vodka on the kitchen table. He poured himself a glass as I just stood and watched.

"Honey, don't you think it's a little early to be hitting the hard stuff?"

Mike picked up the plate of food and threw it at me. He had already started drinking before he got home. His aim was way off and he hit the wall instead.

"You're not my boss. I can drink when I get good and damn ready to! I'm your boss, Sara. I tell you what to do." He grabbed the glass of vodka and attempted to throw it at me, but I ducked out of the way. I set up a plate for Michelle and myself. He even grabbed those plates and threw them against the wall. Most of the plates broke and caused a loud crashing sound as they fell to the floor. That's when he stood up and started grabbing plates and glasses from the kitchen countertop and throwing those as well. I ran out of the room into the living room. I did not want him to hit me. Michelle heard the loud noise and woke up crying.

"You better shut that brat up! Forget this. You made me lose my appetite. I'm going to bed. You get in that kitchen and clean up that mess." Mike walked to the bedroom and politely slammed the door behind him.

"Mommy, Mommy."

"Calm down, baby. Daddy just dropped some dishes. It's OK. I love you. Mommy loves her little angel." Gently rocking

Michelle in my arms, I finally got her to calm down. She was frightened by all the loud noise. I made her a bowl of oatmeal and fed it to her in the living room.

Afterward, I went back into the kitchen to attempt to tackle that mess. My goodness, it looked like a tornado had just hit. I got busy sweeping up broken glass off the floor and wiping eggs and juice from the walls. Then I heard a loud knock on the front door.

"Who is it?"

Someone replied, "The Henderson County police."

Hesitantly, I walked toward the door. When I looked through the peephole, I saw two policemen. I gently opened the door.

"Sara Faraday, we received an anonymous call from someone in the neighborhood saying that they heard loud noises coming from this house. They were afraid that you and your daughter were in some sort of danger."

"Officer, I can assure you that my daughter and I are just fine. I was doing some cleaning in the kitchen, when I accidentally pulled the tablecloth off the kitchen table. All of the dishes fell to the floor and broke."

"Ma'am, is it OK if my partner and I come in and have a look around the house? We don't have a warrant, but then again, if everything is alright like you say it is, then we won't need one. We just want to look through the front door, Mrs. Farraday. If you don't feel comfortable, you can keep the door open at all times."

I told them that was fine. Michelle came walking out of her bedroom toward me. The policemen walked into the kitchen.

"You've got a lot of broken dishes here, ma'am. You accidentally pulled the tablecloth to the floor?"

"Yes, I can be so clumsy at times."

"Looks like someone threw a few of these dishes at the wall or even at somebody." I just stood there smiling. "Mrs. Faraday, where is your husband?"

"He's asleep, officer."

"Did he sleep through the noise?"

"No, he came out to see what was going on, and then, he went back to bed, sir. He works the night shift." I continued to stand there smiling, praying to myself they would soon leave.

"I know your husband. I pulled him over one night for speeding. He had a woman in the car with him. Yeah, he works at that strip club on the outskirts of town. Your husband had a bad attitude that night. Ma'am, is there anything that you'd like to tell us or anything that you would like to report?"

"No, officers. Everything happened just like I said it did," I replied as I slowly wiped away the sweat from my upper lip.

"Well, since you say everything is alright, we're going to get out of here and let you get back to cleaning. We'd like to help you, ma'am, with your kitchen, but we're on duty. "Please don't hesitate to call us if you need anything."

"Thank you, officers, for your concern." I walked the policemen out onto the front porch. I saw my two neighbors, the nosy twins, standing out in their yard. The idea did occur to me that they were the ones who called the police. I must admit, they were kind and generous ladies. Giving Michelle and me cakes, cookies, pies. I'm sure they meant well and were concerned. I waved good morning to the sisters. Just letting them know that everything was alright. As the policemen drove off, I went back inside the house to tackle the kitchen.

CHAPTER ELEVEN:

Five Years of Marriage

My goodness, five years had gone by. All I seemed to be doing was making things worse for my family. Mike was angry all the time. I didn't want to say anything to hurt his feelings. I felt if we could just sit down and talk for a while, then maybe things would be better. I hated myself for making him so miserable. I loved Mike so much. I just couldn't imagine my life without him.

Michelle was in kindergarten already. School was hard, but I finally finished all of my business courses and received my master's degree in business and accounting with a generous amount of help from Edna. She would babysit Michelle in the evening. She also would let me leave at lunchtime to attend some of my classes. I was so proud. I tried to get Mike to attend my graduation, but he said he was too tired from all the late night work.

The day after my graduation, I had planned on driving Michelle to Loxley to see her grandmother at the farm. She had gotten so tall over the years. I packed up her clothes for the weekend. Mama wasn't able to come to my graduation, but she had planned a huge dinner at the farm for family and friends. I couldn't wait to see everyone. Mike was just getting home from his so-called job that morning.

"Hey, Sara. Where are the two of you going?"

"We're going to Loxley for the weekend. Mama wants to visit with Michelle. She called earlier this week, and I told her I would drive down this weekend for a visit."

Mike grabbed my arm. "You don't leave this house unless you ask me first. You didn't tell me you were going anywhere."

I've been going to the farm for years and it hasn't been a problem. What's the problem now?"

He kept squeezing my arm as hard as he could. About five minutes later a car drove up. Some lady came up to the front porch screaming for Mike to open the door. With much hesitation, Mike finally let go of my arm and went to answer the door. The lady was tall and slender with long red hair. She wore a short red dress. She started cursing and yelling.

"Where in the hell is my money, Mike?" She kept pushing him until she pushed her way into the house.

"I don't know what money you're talking about," Mike said.

She slapped Mike across the face several times. "You stay out of my way, Sara," she said to me. "I ain't got no beef with you. Your old man owes me two thousand dollars, and I ain't leaving until the bitch pays me."

"I don't owe you two thousand dollars."

"I made two thousand dollars last night and you stole it from me, Big Mike. I want it back."

Mike slapped the lady as hard as he could, but she was tough. It didn't even faze her. She kneed him in the groin and repeatedly punched him in the face. I couldn't believe what I was seeing. I sat down on the sofa. Those two were going at it, and she was kicking Mike's ass. He finally fell on the floor. Mike had blood coming out of his nose and mouth. She grabbed his wallet from his back pants pocket. She counted out at least $1,800.

"I'll take this for now, you bitch." She threw the wallet on the floor. "Mrs. Farraday, you have a good day now."

She walked out of the house and got into her car. The strangest thing, although she was a pretty woman, I'm not sure if she was really a woman. I wanted to help Mike, but I was afraid. I didn't know if I should call the police or not. I helped him up to the sofa. I got him an ice pack for his nose and mouth.

"Mommy, what's going on?" Michelle was crying. She was so afraid.

"Sweetheart, stay in your room and watch TV. Everything is alright. Keep getting your things together and I'll let you know when it's time to go to the farm."

"But, Mommy, what's wrong with Daddy? I saw that woman hurt him. Is he going to be alright, Mommy?"

"Yes...Baby, he's just sick right now, but I'm gonna help him feel better real soon. Now go into your room and don't worry. Mommy loves you."

"Alright, Mommy."

I gave Michelle a big hug and a kiss as she went back into her room. "Who are you calling, Sara?" Mike asked.

"I'm calling the police."

"No! No police."

"But that woman just came into this house and not only beat you up, she stole your money. We need to report this to the police."

"No damn police. Just help me into the bedroom."

"Let me at least take you to the hospital."

"No. No. No! Just help me into the bedroom."

"Alright."

I helped Mike into the bedroom. I wanted to ask him what had just happened, but I was too afraid. Mike didn't explain anything about who that woman was or even if that was really a woman. He just stayed quiet once I helped him get cleaned up. He lay in the bed moaning out in pain. I called Mama and told her that Mike wasn't feeling good today.

"Hi Mama."

"Hey Sara. I thought you and Michelle would have been here by now. Is something wrong? Oh my goodness, what has Mike done?"

"No, Mama, I'm fine. Mike's not feeling good. He's pretty sick. I think he may have the flu or maybe even pneumonia. He looks real bad. I'm gonna stay here with him. I'm sorry. I know you guys were looking forward to our visit. I'm going to stay at home and take care of him."

"But, Sara, what about your graduation dinner? I was planning on cooking you all of your favorites. If Mike is that sick, then maybe he needs to go to the hospital. Sweetie, I just hate that you're not going to be here this weekend."

"Mama, I am so sorry. Trust me; I didn't plan any of this. But Mike is just so sick."

"Yeah, you already said that. Look, I'm sorry for being selfish. I just don't want to miss out on any opportunity to visit with my two girls. We can postpone the dinner for another time."

"Thank you, Mama. You know, spring break will be starting in a couple of weeks. I can bring Michelle down to visit for an entire week."

"Now that sounds like a great idea."

"Michelle will love that idea also. Well, I better get back to Mike. I'm so sorry. Please apologize to everyone for me. I love you all."

"I love you too, Sara. Keep me informed about Mike's condition. Talk to you later, baby."

"Goodbye, Mama."

"Will you get off that damn phone and give me something for pain?" Mike yelled from the bedroom. "I'm hurting like hell over here."

"Let me see what's in the medicine cabinet. We've got Tylenol, aspirin, sleeping pills."

"Yeah, sleeping pills, give me three of those and five aspirin."

"Mike, you don't need all that."

"Sara, I am in pain! Do what I tell you to do!" And that's exactly what I did; I gave Mike three sleeping pills and five aspirin just like he wanted. I told Michelle that her daddy wasn't feeling well, so we weren't going to the farm this weekend, but she could spend the entire week of spring break in Loxley.

She was so happy. Mike eventually fell asleep. I figured he'd be out for the rest of the day and probably tomorrow also.

I decided to take Michelle to Edna's house for the weekend. Still somewhat in shock, I told her what happened, and I didn't want Michelle in the house just in case that woman came back to get the rest of her money from Mike.

"Yeah, Mike's going to end up in a bad situation dealing with Billy and that club," Joe replied. "What happened to your arms, Sara?" I had forgotten about the bruises on my arms.

"I picked up a heavy box the wrong way and it bruised my arm."

"Sara, when are you going to stop making excuses? Edna and I know that Mike has been beating on you."

"He's just under so much pressure right now. Things will get better," I replied. Joe caught me off guard when he asked me about my arms.

Something inside of me wanted to tell the truth, but I didn't know how. I had been lying now for the past five years. Something in me wanted to scream, but I couldn't. What would they say about me? Would they feel sorry for me? I didn't want people to feel sorry for me. Maybe they would call me stupid. I needed to make my marriage work. I'd never known how it feels to have both parents. I wanted my children to have parents, a mom and a dad. All of these thoughts just started racing inside my head. I didn't feel like talking anymore.

"Edna and Joe, take good care of Michelle. I'll be back tomorrow to pick her up."

"Be careful, Sara."

I drove back home to check on Mike. I wanted him so desperately to tell me what happened, but I knew I couldn't push the issue. When I drove up to the house, the neighbors were standing in their front yard watering their plants. I admired their beautiful flowers. Michelle liked the two sisters. They loved to bake cookies and cakes. Very pleasant ladies, just a little on the nosy side. They had no children of their own.

I guess they felt as if they had to watch out for Michelle and me. They had to be at least in their seventies. I spoke to them as I walked toward the front porch.

Gently I opened the door and eased into the house. Mike was still in bed. While I was tiptoeing around in the bedroom, I noticed Mike's wallet sticking halfway out of his pocket. I slowly eased it out of his jeans and took it into the kitchen. I started to feel bad about sneaking through his wallet, but I had to attempt to find out what he was up to. I slowly scanned through his wallet. There were a few business cards that read "For a good time go to Big Billy's Lounge, Big Mike will take care of you." The card also had a business number and a cell phone number. That was strange; Mike told me he didn't have a cell phone. He had five hundred dollars hidden away between two letters. I peeped back into the bedroom to make sure he was still asleep. I took the letters out of his wallet and started to read them. One of them was from his father.

Dear Mike, I heard from Edna that you were working for Billy Lucas at his club. You know that I'm not happy about that at all. Billy Lucas is not a good man. Everywhere he goes trouble is soon to follow. Prostitution, drugs, strippers, is that the kind of life you want to live? Mike, I'm sorry, I know after all these years you felt that I blamed you for your mother's death, and maybe in some strange way I did. I want something I never had before, I want my son. I've always been there, but I haven't been there for you. We need to talk. Don't take it out on Sara, Mike, take it out on me. I'm the one who let you down, not her. It was me. Please call me. I want us to get together so that we can talk about this once and for all. I love you, son.

The letter brought tears to my eyes. All of a sudden, I heard heavy breathing. As I turned around, Mike was standing right behind me. I gently smiled. I couldn't think of anything to say. I had the letter in my hand still that his dad had sent him.

"What the hell are you doing, Sara?"

"Baby, I was looking for the number to your job. I thought I'd call them and let them know that you were sick and you wouldn't be coming in tonight. Your eye is still bruised and swollen. Maybe you should stay home tonight and get some rest." I slowly rubbed his chest.

"Did you call them?"

"No, sweetie. You've got so many cards here, I couldn't figure out which number to call."

I neatly folded the letters and stuck them back into his wallet and pretended I had one of his nightclub cards. "Don't call anyone. I'm going to work. You didn't have to steal my wallet."

He slowly started to walk toward me. I felt in the pit of my stomach that he was going to hit me. "Mike, don't you remember that the redheaded woman threw your wallet on the floor? I picked it up and laid it on the kitchen counter."

I gently kissed his lips and prayed that he wouldn't remember that I picked it up earlier that morning and put it back into his pants pocket. "Here's your wallet, baby. I'll fix you something good for dinner. You go back and get some rest."

I walked over to the refrigerator and started taking out some chicken and potatoes. I could feel Mike's eyes staring at me, just watching my every move. I got a cold beer from the refrigerator and gave it to him.

"This will help you to relax, honey."

Everything seemed to be alright. Mike took the beer and started walking toward the bedroom. Suddenly the doorbell rang. Mike went into the bedroom saying, "If it's for me, tell them I'm not here."

He slammed the bedroom door and locked it. I went to the front door and opened it. Uncle Joe was standing there. "Hi, Joe. Is Michelle alright?."

"Michelle's just fine. I need to talk to that husband of yours."

"Joe, I don't think that's a good idea right now. He's very sick. Maybe the two of you can talk some other time."

"Where is he, Sara? Is he in the bedroom hiding?"

Mike opened the bedroom door. "Look, old man, I ain't got no beef with you right now, so let's keep it that way."

"Mike, I ain't no fool. I heard that you've been pimping women and men out at Billy's club. You can't lead that kind of life with a wife and a child. Sara's a good woman. She deserves a man that's going to love her and treat her like a queen, not someone who beats on her."

"Who told you that, Uncle Joe?" Mike asked. "I've never hit Sara a day in her life."

"Save those lies for someone else."

Uncle Joe said that the majority of the town knew that Mike had been abusing me. Tears started to roll down my face. I felt so embarrassed and ashamed. Mike turned around and walked back toward the bedroom door. Joe grabbed his arm. "Mike, don't walk away from me when I'm talking to you."

Mike snatched his arm away from Joe and said, "I don't want to start nothing with you today, old man. You need to get out of here and mind your own business."

"Sara and I get along just fine."

I was praying that Joe would leave. Both of them were very angry. "You have a good day, Uncle Joe, and get the hell out of my house."

Mike went into the bedroom and slammed the door as hard as he could behind him. Joe started walking toward the bedroom door. "Don't walk away from me, Mike."

I ran up to him. "Joe, please, just let it go. I appreciate what you're trying to do, but you're only making things worse. Let Mike think about what you said."

I begged Joe to just go home as I fought to hold back my tears. I did not want him to see me cry. "I'm going to cook dinner. I'll come by tomorrow afternoon to pick up Michelle. Everything will be alright, I promise."

Joe did not say a word. He gave me a big hug and walked out the front door. I stood in the doorway until Joe drove off down the street. I shut the front door. I was so upset as I walked into the kitchen. If someone had offered me a rock, I probably would have crawled under it. But I knew I had to pull myself together for the sake of my daughter. I needed to start cooking before Mike got up from his nap. I washed my hands and started to remove the chicken from the plastic container. All of a sudden, someone grabbed me from behind. It was Mike. I didn't hear him come out of the bedroom. He grabbed my hair and pulled it as hard as he could, forcing me down to the floor on my knees. "Why are you telling them what goes on in our house?"

"Mike, please don't hurt me. I didn't say anything to anyone, I promise."

"You're lying!" Mike dragged me across the kitchen floor by my hair.

"Mike, please stop."

I was in so much pain. I just knew he was going to pull my hair completely out of my head. He dragged me over by the front door. "You've got no business telling people what goes on in my house. Everything is your freaking fault."

"Mike, I'm so sorry. Let's just talk about it later. You need some rest, honey. You're just tired."

Mike slung open the front door. He dragged me out onto the front porch.

"I can't get no rest, so you stay outside so I can get some sleep!" Mike yelled at me.

He continued to drag me down the three steps onto the cement walkway. He finally let go of my hair. He went back into the house and locked the front door. I quickly stood up from the walkway, before the neighbors came outside. I was in so much pain. My head was hurting so bad. I felt as if the whole world was spinning around—I was just that dizzy.

I sat on the front porch for a while. My back and rear end felt as if all of the skin had been rubbed off. Wow, what I wouldn't have done for a bottle of aspirin right about then. I stood up slowly and started to walk toward the street. Maybe the fresh air would help me feel better. I missed the fresh air back in Loxley. I decided I'd go to the park. I was just glad that it wasn't wintertime.

I found a napkin lying in the street. "Lord, I hope this napkin is safe." I glanced around to see if anyone was watching as I picked up the napkin to wash the tears from my face. Boy, was I hurting. The walk would help with the stiffness and pain.

CHAPTER TWELVE:

Pregnant Again

Walking calmly, trying not to attract any attention, I suddenly started to feel nauseated. I hoped I hadn't injured myself. I walked over to one of the park benches. There was a smell of barbecue and hamburgers in the air. It made me even more nauseated. I sat down slowly onto the bench. A young lady and her baby were also sitting at the other end of the bench. She was a pretty baby. She reminded me of Michelle when she was born. All tiny and fresh, smelling like the first day of spring. The park was full of children playing, joggers jogging, people walking their dogs, and bike riders. The strangest thing happened. The young lady sharing the bench with me asked if I was pregnant. Maybe she asked me that because I was staring at her baby.

I quickly replied, "No, I'm not pregnant."

"The reason I asked you that is because you've got that rosy look on your cheeks like I had when I was pregnant with my little Amanda," the young lady replied.

"Is that your baby's name, Amanda?"

"Yes, ma'am, I named her after my grandmother. You know, you do have that pregnant woman's glow. Well, I've got to take Amanda home for her evening nap. You take care of yourself, miss."

"You too, and take care of little Amanda."

I sat there for a while thinking about what the young lady said. Could I be pregnant? Wow, come to think of it, I couldn't remember when I had my last period. Nauseated, tired all of time, could I be pregnant? I had to get to the drugstore and buy a pregnancy test. I got up from the bench and started jogging down the street. I was still sore, but I had to get to the house. It hurt too bad to jog, so I slowed to a walk.

Finally, I got home. It seemed like hours, but it was only a ten-minute walk. I went up to the front door and turned the knob, but I had forgotten Mike locked the door. But what Mike didn't know was that I kept a spare key under one of the flowerpots on the front porch. I slowly unlocked the front door and let myself in, staying as quiet as possible. I definitely did not want to wake up Mike. I grabbed my purse from the living room sofa, gently walked back to the front door, and let myself out. I cranked my car and backed out of the driveway. I looked in my rearview mirror as I drove down the street. I did not see Mike. Thank goodness.

I went to the local drugstore about three miles from the house. As I rushed into the store, my cell phone rang. It was my mama. I didn't have time to talk to her right now, but I answered the phone with my usual cheerful and happy voice. "Hi, Mama."

"Hello, Sara. How are you?"

"I'm just fine, Mama."

"How is Mike feeling?"

"He's resting, Mama, but I'm at the drugstore right now."

"Is there anything serious going on with him?"

"He's just coming down with a cold. I was buying some Tylenol."

"Sara, Janie and I are driving down to visit with you tomorrow. We've got to come out that way and pick up some supplies. We'll probably stop by around lunchtime and visit with you all. Mike's father has been trying to reach him. Tell him to give his dad a call."

My mind was a hundred miles away from the conversation. All I wanted was to buy a pregnancy test. "That's good, Mama."

"Sara, what are you doing? You sound like you're out of breath."

"No, I'm fine. I'm just walking through the store looking for some feminine items, that's all. I'll see you tomorrow. Mama, I love you."

"Alright, Sara, I love you too, honey. I hope Mike feels better. Talk with you later."

"Bye, Mama."

"Goodbye, Sara."

I hated to rush Mama off the phone, but I had to find that pregnancy test. I guessed they were pretty much all the same. I'd never done this before.

"May I help you, miss?" one of the pharmacy assistants asked.

"I just wanted to buy a pregnancy test."

"This is a good one and it's not that expensive. Would that be cash or credit card?"

I placed a credit card on the counter. The pharmacy assistant looked at my credit card and said, "Sara Farraday, are you by chance married to Mike Farraday?" I hesitated before I answered.

"Yeah," I said slowly.

"My sister works for him at Big Billy's Lounge."

Out of pure curiosity, I just had to ask, "What kind of work does your sister do?"

"Well, let's just say she makes twice as much money in one week than I make in two weeks. Mrs. Faraday, good luck with your test."

I smiled and quickly grabbed the bag and went out the door. I saw a McDonald's next to the drugstore. Glancing around to see if anyone was looking, I went into the restaurant's bathroom. There was no way I could wait to get home. I had to know right now whether or not I was pregnant. Carefully

I followed the instructions on the box. Those three minutes seemed like three hours.

It was positive. I was pregnant.

I walked back to my car and just sat there for a while. It was getting late. I had to hurry up and get home before Mike realized that I had left the house. As I drove into the driveway, I hid my purse under the front seat. I put the spare key back under the flowerpot on the front porch. I slipped my car keys into my back pocket and then sat on the front steps. I sat there for at least ten minutes.

Mike came to the door and opened it. I stood up quickly. He walked into the living room. Slowly I walked into the house and shut the door behind me. Mike was dressed for work. I went into the kitchen and started to put away the food that I had gotten out earlier. Mike grabbed me and forced me down to the floor. He told me that I needed to do my wifely duties. I didn't fight him. He unbuckled my belt and pulled down my jeans and panties. He pulled down his pants and lay on top of me. He kissed my lips, and put his hand under my shirt, touching my breast. We were both in so much pain. He tried to have sex with me, but he couldn't. He kept trying, but he couldn't have an erection. He finally decided to stop. He stood up.

"Damn you, Sara. You've got me so stressed out that I can't even get a hard-on. You don't even turn me on anymore."

He pulled up his pants. "My back is killing me. I'm going to work; you better have me something ready to eat when I get home in the morning. If you can do that right."

He walked out of the kitchen down the hallway to the front door. I got up slowly. My hip was hurting from where Mike had dragged me out of the house. He finally left the house. I felt dirty, so I decided to take a hot shower. Maybe it would help me feel better.

I still couldn't believe I was pregnant. I wanted to go to the emergency room to confirm the results of the home pregnancy test. That sounded a little stupid, going to the hospital just to have a pregnancy test done. I could make an appointment on Monday to see my doctor. Standing in the shower, just letting the warm water flow down my back felt so good. It brought a smile to my face and joy to my heart, knowing that I was carrying a new life inside of me again. What would Mike say? When Michelle was born, he was excited. Hopefully this baby would be a boy. I knew that Mike would love to have a little Michael Jr., but then again, what if I was wrong? Nonsense. I was sure after five years of marriage; he'd love to have another baby. I wasn't going to think about it until I knew for sure if I was pregnant.

I had to get out of the shower and start cooking some dinner. I felt nice and comfortable wearing my silk pajamas. I tried to decide between taking some aspirin for my back or taking Tylenol. I took the Tylenol, since I was probably pregnant. Man, I wanted to have a little boy. That's just what the marriage needed for us to get back on track, I thought. I knew Mike didn't mean to hurt me. He had so much on his mind, and trying to work a night shift, I knew that he was under a lot of pressure. I wondered if I should suggest that we go on a long vacation during the summer. Mama could watch Michelle, and Mike and I could go on a cruise or something. We never had had a real honeymoon. I was so excited. My goodness, I thought, it could be the perfect answer to making our marriage work.

The chicken and rice smelled good. It was Mike's favorite dish. I decided to make a banana pudding for desert. It would be my dinner and his breakfast.

The chicken was finally finished. I washed all the dishes. Everything was neatly put away. At nine o'clock I went into the bedroom and tucked myself into bed. It had been a long day. All I wanted to do was get some sleep.

Morning came so fast. I loved to see the sun shining through the windows. The sun was my personal alarm clock. I could still feel the soreness in my back as I got out of bed. I must admit, I had a pretty good night's sleep. My stomach felt a little queasy this morning. It was probably my nerves, more so than the pregnancy. I took another warm shower before getting dressed for the day. It was about eight o'clock, but Mike wasn't home yet. He evidently was running late, since he was usually home about seven thirty or eight. I called Edna to check on Michelle.

"Good morning, Edna, this is Sara, I was just calling to see if Michelle was behaving herself."

"Good morning, Sara. Michelle had a great night. She slept like a little angel. We're about to have breakfast right now. Would you like to talk to her?"

"No. You all go ahead and have breakfast."

"Sara, we're gonna be out for the day at church services. We'll bring Michelle back later this evening, if that's alright with you?"

"Sure, Edna, that sounds just fine. Give Michelle a big hug and kiss for me, and I'll see you all later today."

"Goodbye, Sara, you have a blessed day."

Five past ten, Mike still wasn't home. I heated up his dinner, hoping that by the time it was hot, he would be home. Everything was nice and warm. I let his plate stay wrapped up on the stove. It was unusual for him to run this late getting home from work.

As I sat in the living room, I heard a car driving into the driveway. I figured it had to be Mike. I couldn't wait for him to get inside the house. Should I tell him? No…I would wait until I knew for sure. Mike rushed into the house. I stood up from the recliner ready to give him a big hug and kiss.

"Someone told me that you might be pregnant. Are you pregnant, Sara?"

I was literally in shock. I had no idea that he practically already knew. Mike kept walking closer and closer to me. I slowly backed up gently as I asked, "Who told you that, honey?"

"It doesn't matter who told me. Is it true? Are you pregnant?"

"I'm not sure."

"Either you are or you're not."

I could hear Mike's heart beating as I stood in front of him. The anger was slowly building up. I tried to look him in the eyes, but I couldn't take my eyes off of his fist. The closer he walked toward me, the tighter his fist seemed to get.

"I took the drugstore pregnancy test, but I haven't seen a doctor yet. So I'm not sure."

Mike's voice became louder with every word he spoke. He kept staring directly into my eyes. I felt in the pit of my stomach that he was going to hit me.

"What did the damn thing say, Sara?" Mike pushed the recliner chair out of the way. I could feel the heat coming from his breath as he stood directly in my face. Slowly trying to back away, I started to smile.

"Baby, the test said positive, but you know half the time those things aren't accurate."

Before I could finish my sentence, Mike grabbed my shoulders and began shaking me.

"I thought you were on birth control pills. How can you get pregnant taking birth control pills?" Practically screaming at me now, he just kept shaking me harder and harder.

"I may have missed a couple of pills."

"What do you mean, you may have missed a couple of pills? What do you mean?"

"Mike, please. You're hurting me."

Mike just kept screaming, "You're trying to set me up, just like you did before."

"Please keep your voice down, the neighbors will hear you."

"I don't give a damn about the neighbors. I'm tired of women setting me up all the time."

Mike took the back of his right hand and slapped me across the right side of my face. I held onto the recliner chair to keep from falling to the floor. Mike was filled with rage as if he were turning into some type of monster.

"Please, Mike, stop."

He slapped me again, twice as hard as before. My whole body became numb. I fell over the recliner chair onto the living room floor. A few drops of blood fell from my nose and mouth. Crying and pleading, I begged him to stop. "You're gonna hurt the baby."

"I don't care if I kill it."

I kept hearing what sounded like a car door closing. Mike was yelling so loud, I thought maybe I was just hearing things. He continued to stand in front of me. He was just about to kick me in the stomach when we heard a loud knock at the front door. Neither one of us said anything, nor did we move.

"Sara, are you in there?" Oh my goodness, it was Janie's voice. I forgot Mama and Janie said they were coming by today for a visit. Mike recognized the voice and immediately helped me up from the floor. He cleaned the blood from my face with a paper towel lying on the living room table.

"We'll be right there," Mike yelled out. He whispered into my ear, "You better not say a word about this."

Mike opened the door.

"What's going on? We heard loud yelling and screaming when we got out of the truck. Sara, what's going on?" Julia said.

"Hello, in-laws. We were just having a little lover's quarrel, that's all," Mike replied. Mama ran over and hugged me. My back was hurting so bad that I darn near screamed out in pain. Janie walked over to me slowly while I was hugging Mama. She pulled up my shirt and looked at my back.

"Oh my goodness. What is this? Sara, you've got bruises all over your back."

She then glanced up at my face.

"Your nose is bleeding. What has this animal been doing to you?"

Mama looked at Mike. "What have you been doing to my daughter, Michael?"

I could see that anger building in Janie's eyes. I knew I had to think of something fast to say.

"Mama, it was me. You know how clumsy I am. I fell out of the swing on the front porch. Yeah, the darn thing threw me so hard, I fell from the porch down to the ground. Man, that was a hard fall."

"Yeah, just like when Sharon Howser fell off Mike's front porch," Janie said. "You do remember Sharon Howser, don't you, Mike?"

"Now you look here, Janie, I'm tired of you sticking your nose in our business," Mike said.

Janie ran up to Mike and began choking him. She hit him in the face with her fist. I knew if I didn't do something, she would kill him. I could never forgive myself if my own sister killed my husband. I grabbed Janie and pushed her. She bumped into the wall. A tear slowly rolled down her cheek.

"How could you stick up for that creep? Sara, I'm your sister. I love you. That jerk is gonna end up killing you one day."

"Janie, stop it! Mike isn't perfect, but neither am I. We can work together and save our marriage. I know that we can. Please, Janie, don't make any problems for us."

Oh my goodness, what had I just done? Janie had so much hurt in her eyes. I had just destroyed the relationship that I had with my only sister. Just then there was another loud knock at the front door.

"Open the door, please, it's the police."

Janie immediately went to the door. "Oh, you're going to jail this time for what you did to Sara."

Janie told the police to come in and arrest that man, pointing at Mike. "He just beat up my sister. She's got bruises and a bloody nose to prove it."

There were two police officers, one male and the other a female.

The male cop asked me, "Is it true? Did this man hit you?"

Before I could say anything, the female cop looked at Mike and said, "Sir, how did you get those bruises on your face and neck?" Mike still had several bruises on his face from when he got beat up by one of his so-called girls.

"Sara and I both were sitting outside on the front porch swing. I should have fixed it years ago. The darn thing is about forty years old. The chain gave away from the roof of the house, and we both ended up falling from the porch onto the concrete walkway. It was a real nasty fall for both of us, wasn't it, Sara?"

Janie looked at me. "Sara, you don't have to lie. We will protect you. Please tell the police what happened."

This seemed like the hardest decision I'd ever had to make in my life. I stood frozen in my tracks. My lips wouldn't move.

"Sara, they can take him to jail," Janie said.

I began to think about it, but again, before I could say anything, the policewoman made her comments. "If there is any domestic violence going on in the home, the law is we have to take you both in for questioning. You both may be spending the night in a jail cell."

No jails. I couldn't get locked up. Who would take care of Michelle and what about me being pregnant? I immediately thought about what she said.

"Yes. Mike is right. We were both swinging on the front porch when the entire thing just fell to the ground. We both got pretty banged up. That's why we're so bruised up."

"Who fixed the swing?" the male officer asked.

"Sir?"

"I said, who fixed the swing? It's hanging outside."

"We had it fixed this morning," Mike said. "I didn't want my little girl coming home trying to swing on that broken thing."

I don't think the male policeman believed anything that we had said. Mama was so scared. I could see the fear in her eyes. I hated this whole situation. I didn't like lying to my family.

"Sara, are you sure everything is alright?" Mama asked.

"I'm just a little sore from the fall, Mama, but I'll live."

"That's what you think," Janie replied. "She needs to go to the hospital. My sister is hurt pretty bad."

The police offered to call an ambulance, but Mama said that she and Janie would take me to the emergency room.

"If there is nothing going on here, then we'll be on our way," the female officer said. She handed a card to Mike. "If you have any problems, please don't hesitate to call me."

I had the feeling that he had called her before in the past, and it wasn't a professional call. They looked around the house and saw that everything was in place. Dinner for Mike was still warming on the stove. "You folks have a good day." The policeman said.

They both left. Janie looked at me as if she could rip the skin off my body with her bare hands.

"Why didn't you tell them what happened?"

"Janie, I don't want to go to jail. You heard what that cop said. I really did fall outside just like Mike said. I'm not lying."

I hated this. I never thought I would have to lie to my own mother. "Sara, I'm gonna take you to the hospital just to make sure you're alright."

"Mama—"

"Don't say another word! You go outside and get in that truck!" Mama was angry. She had never yelled at me that way before. I grabbed my purse from the living room table and walked outside to the truck.

"I hate you, Mike Faraday, and one day you will get what's coming to you," Janie said. Mama, Janie, and I got into the truck.

"Did I hear Mike say something about you being pregnant?" Mama asked.

"I took a pregnancy test, Mama, but it was one of those drugstore tests. I tested positive. I'm going to make an appointment with my doctor on Monday."

Why did I say that the test was positive? Mama and Janie started to yell at me.

"How could you let Mike hurt you and you're pregnant? What's wrong with you? Have you lost your mind?" Janie said.

All I could do was sit in between the two of them and cry. The overwhelming feeling of shame and embarrassment was just too much for me to bear. What could I say? Should I just let them yell at me without even defending myself? The tears rolled down harder and harder. I couldn't say anything. More or less, I was afraid to say anything.

We finally drove up to the emergency room door. I hate hospitals. The only time I ever had to go to one was when I gave birth to Michelle. They are for sick people. I wasn't sick. I hurt like heck, but I wasn't sick. Mama and I got out of the truck. Janie went to look for a parking space. I hesitantly walked to the information desk.

"Ma'am, do you need a wheelchair?" the hospital clerk asked.

"No, I think I can make it." I hated people feeling sorry for me. That's the last thing I ever wanted. The clerk took all of my insurance information and told me to take a seat in the waiting room.

"Ma'am, the nurse will call you into the back as soon as a room becomes available."

Before I could even walk away from the desk, I overheard a couple of the nurses talking about me.

"Stacy, did you see her face? What is she here for?"

"She said she fell off the front porch, but if you ask me, I think she fell off her husband's fist."

"She can barely walk. I asked her if she needed a wheelchair when they drove up, but she said no."

"I don't know why women allow themselves to get hit like that. I couldn't be in a relationship with a man that hits me all of the time. I'd probably kill him in his sleep."

"Brenda, it's just not that simple. When Darryl was beating up on me five years ago, I couldn't even discuss it with my family or anyone. All I could do was pretend that everything was alright. I did not want to involve my family, and I definitely did not want them to know about the hell I was going through. Darryl told me he loved me. I believed him. It took me three years to figure out that hitting someone is not showing that you love them."

"What made you finally decide to leave him?"

"I was trapped. He became so paranoid. Every time I left the apartment, he swore I was going out to meet a man. He even accused me of having sex with my own cousin, Jerry. It was as if he turned into Dr. Jekyll and Mr. Hyde. The man I fell in love with was gone, forever. He didn't want me to pay any bills. He wanted all of the money. I couldn't talk to my family or my friends. One night after he just finished beating me, he went to the store. I waited until he was gone and I left the apartment. I ran down the street and I never looked back. The only things I took with me were the clothes on my back. Nothing else mattered. I never saw Darryl again. You remember that girl they brought in here about six years ago? The one that had been hit in the head with the hammer by her old man? I looked at her body; her face haunted me every night. All I could see was the fear in her big brown eyes. They were asking for help, but it was too late. Domestic violence killed her. If I had stayed with Darryl, I just knew I would have ended up the same way, in a morgue. I haven't dreamed about that girl in five years."

"Stacy, you never said anything. In all the years that I've known you, why didn't you tell me what Darryl was doing to you?"

"Trust me, that's not the kind of thing that someone wants to sit around and talk about at a dinner party. I just didn't want people to know what was going on in my life. I was embarrassed and afraid. I thought things would get better, but they never did. Domestic violence is a disease, and if you're not careful, it will kill you."

"Paging Dr. Randall to ICU," was announced over the hospital PA. I quickly went to my seat before the clerks saw me standing there.

"I've got to get back to work, Stacy. I'll see you for lunch."

"Alright. Let me go see what's up with Dr. Randall. See you at seven o'clock."

When I sat down in the waiting room, my cell phone started to ring. It was Mike. It rung for a few minutes before I reluctantly went into the bathroom to answer it.

"Sara. Sara, I know that you can hear me. Look, you don't have to talk, but I have something to say to you. Please don't hang up. Sara, I'm sorry. I just don't know what came over me, baby. Don't forget how much I love you and Michelle. You take care and let me know what the doctor says about the baby."

I just held the phone. For the first time in my life, I didn't feel like talking to Mike Faraday. "Honey, don't be mad. I had to lie to the cops. Sara, I didn't want them to take you to jail. I couldn't do that to you. Please call me."

"I'll call you after I see the doctor."

"That's my girl. Oh, by the way, dinner was delicious."

After I hung up my cell phone, I walked back to the waiting room. Janie had finally parked the truck. She came running into the hospital like a witch riding on a broomstick.

"Sara, you listen to me, you've got to tell the police that Mike did this to you, especially if you are pregnant."

"Janie, please, just leave it alone. I fell down just like I said. If the police find out that anything went on, they will take me to jail. The courts will take Michelle from me. I can't let that happen."

I didn't want to talk about any of this, especially in a hospital waiting room.

"Honey, Mama and I will protect you from Mike. You know that we won't let anything happen to Michelle."

The nurse finally came into the waiting room. "Sara Farraday to exam room two please."

Mama and Janie stood up. "I'm sorry, ladies, only the patient is allowed to go into the exam room right now. I will come back out after the doctor has seen the patient to let you know when you can go back to visit with her."

Boy, was I relieved to get away from Janie and her badgering. The nurse led me into a tiny room with a stretcher. It smelled like Betadine and felt like an icebox.

"Hi, my name is Nancy. I'll be your nurse for the day. What brings you to the ER?"

I spoke low. "I think I might be pregnant and I accidentally fell off the front porch."

"When was the last time you had your period?"

"I think it was a couple of months ago. I've had so much on my mind that I lost track."

"Did you trip over something on the porch?"

"My husband and I were swinging. See, the house is about thirty years old. We have a porch swing that we occasionally sit on. I guess it just couldn't take the weight of both of us swinging and it fell down on the porch. When it fell, my husband and I both fell off the porch onto the concrete walkway."

"Oh my goodness, that sounds like it had to hurt."

"Trust me, it did. You don't know just how bad it hurts."

"Well, first, I'm going to need you to change into this gown. Please remove all of your clothing and leave the gown open in the back. I'm also going to need a urine sample. Your blood pressure is a little elevated. Are you on any medications?"

"No. I was taking birth control pills, but I think I missed a few doses."

I didn't want to take off my clothes. My body was all black and blue. I was so embarrassed. What if they wouldn't believe me?

"Nurse, do I have to take off everything?"

"Yes, ma'am, it's hospital procedure. I'm going to give you some privacy, but as soon as you are finished, please take this cup into the bathroom across the hall for your urine specimen. Here's the sample kit. Wipe yourself from front to back with the moisture cloth. Start urinating, and in the middle of the stream collect as much urine in the sample cup as possible. You can leave it in the specimen holder in the bathroom. The doctor will be in as soon as possible."

I took off my clothes and put on the hospital gown. I left the urine specimen in the bathroom. I went back into that cold exam room. Darn, why did it have to be so cold? You could probably have stored meat in there and it would get frostbite. I lay on the stretcher and covered myself with a sheet, wishing for a blanket. There were so many people here. The weekends must be the busiest days in the emergency room. I lay on that stretcher for so long, I fell asleep.

"Mrs. Farraday. Hi, I'm Dr. Jones."

Wow, he almost scared me to death. I was pleased to see a male doctor. Maybe he wouldn't ask so many stupid questions.

The nurse also walked in. "Mrs. Farraday, I need to collect some blood to send to the lab."

"Well, you are pregnant according to the test," the doctor said, as he kept looking down at my chart. "I also noticed your blood pressure is a little elevated. I'm going to need to examine you. I heard you also had a pretty nasty fall earlier today. I need you to remove the top of your gown, please, and cover your lower body with the sheet."

He helped me pull down my gown. He didn't say anything, but I knew he couldn't help but see the bruises all over my body. Stevie Wonder could have seen those black and blues. He asked me about the bruises that I had on the stomach, my arms, and my back. I reminded him again that I fell off the front porch.

"What about all of the old yellow bruises? Did you fall off the porch last week and the week before that as well?"

All I could do was hold my head down in shame and say no. He was thorough with his examination. He left no stone unturned. I was checked from head to toe.

"Well, so far nothing seems to be broken," the doctor said as he looked me straight into the eyes—staring into my very soul. "You will definitely be sore for a while. This big bruise on your left side is pretty deep. It will take a few weeks to heal. I don't think any damage was done as far your pregnancy is concerned, but I want you to have an ultrasound done before you leave. Your bloodwork and your urine look OK. Please remember to drink more milk or eat more dairy products. Your calcium level was a little low. I suggest you also make an appointment with your gynecologist as soon as possible. From the feel of your uterus, it appears that you may be at least seven to eight weeks pregnant. The nurse will take you down to radiology to have your ultrasound done and they can tell you exactly how far along you are. After your ultrasound you are free to leave. I'm going to write you a prescription for some antibiotics to prevent any type of infection. "Oh, Mrs. Farraday, I'd watch out for your front porch if I were you, it seems to be pretty wicked."

Dr. Jones just smiled and walked out of the room as if he knew I was lying the entire time. The nurse told me that they were so backed up in the radiology department, it would be best if I tried to schedule a visit with my own doctor the next day. She said they would do an ultrasound there at the office. She was nice, and even recommended her own gynecologist, Dr. Susan Blake.

"Now don't forget to make that appointment Mrs.Farraday. Here's her number."

"Thank you so much. I will call the office first thing in the morning."

I got dressed. Then came the hard part, going out there to face Mama and Janie.

"Sara, are you alright?" Mama asked. "What did the doctor say?"

"Nothing's broken Mama. I've just got some bumps and bruises, but they will heal up pretty soon."

"What about the baby? Are you pregnant?"

"Yes. The doctor said that I was probably seven or eight weeks along, but he wasn't sure. I'll have to make an appointment with my gynecologist tomorrow. It's been such a long day, can the two of you just please take me home?"

"Home! For what! To get your ass kicked again by Mike?" Janie asked. She was still angry that I didn't call the police.

"Janie, go get the truck," my mother said.

"Mama, please, talk some sense in to her."

"Janie, I said go get the truck so we can get your sister out of here."

"Yes, ma'am."

Mama and I stood at the door waiting for Janie to bring the truck around. I wasn't looking forward to getting back into that truck with the two of them. I couldn't help but feel that everything would get better. Mike just needed to calm down and let the alcohol wear off. Having another baby was a good idea right now. I stepped up to get into the truck; Janie looked at me as if she could put her hands around my throat and choke the life out of my body. I was almost afraid to climb in and sit next to her.

The drive home was strange. No one said a word. That made me nervous. I could just imagine what they were both thinking about me. We finally arrived at the house. Janie drove up into the driveway. I was relieved. I couldn't stand to be in that truck a minute longer. Mama and I got out of the truck.

"Sara, I love you, and you don't have to put up with this type of treatment. I'm always there for you and Michelle."

"Mama, let's go!" Janie said. "Sara doesn't want our help. All she cares about is Mike."

I held back my tears. "Thank you, Mama. I appreciate you and Janie taking me to the hospital, but I think I'll be alright."

"Janie and I are gonna drive down to Edna's house to visit with Michelle. You take care of yourself, young lady. Love you."

I couldn't help myself. The tears just started to roll down my face. I wanted to be so brave, but I couldn't. "I'll call you tomorrow, Mama. I love you too—both of you."

Mama gave me a big hug. She got into the truck. Janie didn't even look at me. She drove off fast, as if the devil himself were chasing her. I stood on the walkway in the front of the house. My neighbors, the Peck sisters, were sitting on their porch.

"Sara, are you alright?"

"Yes, Ms. Abigail. I'm just fine."

"Your husband left the house about an hour ago," Amanda said. "He left with the man that drives the black truck."

I had seen that guy before. He never came into the house; he only drove into the yard and blew his horn for Mike to come outside. The sisters admitted that they called the police. I know that they just didn't want me to get hurt. Since neither of them had any children, I was the daughter that they never gave birth to. I did appreciate their concern.

"You ladies have a good day."

"Take care, Sara."

CHAPTER THIRTEEN:

Everything Will Get Better

I walked inside the house. I had never felt so alone before in my life. I tried to do some cleaning in the living room, but I became so overwhelmed with grief, all I could do was just lie on the floor and start crying. I must have lain there for at least an hour before getting up. I decided I would call Edna to see if it was alright for Michelle to spend the night. I didn't know what kind of mood Mike would be in when he got home. None of this was her fault. She shouldn't have to suffer for the mistakes that grownups make.

Alright, Sara, get it together and put on your happy face, I told myself—yet again, pretending that everything was fine and dandy as usual. I started to dial the phone. I'm sure Mama and Janie had already arrived and filled Edna and Joe in on everything that had happened. I hoped Edna would answer the phone. I just didn't feel like receiving another lecture from Joe.

"Hello."

"Hi, Edna. It's me, Sara."

"Sara, how are you, sweetie?"

"Well, let's just say I've had a long day. How's Michelle doing?"

"She's doing just fine. As a matter of fact, we were just getting ready to sit down and have dinner. Sara, your mother and sister stopped by the house. I'm not going to put my two cents worth in, but always remember, if you need anything, Joe and I are always here for you and your daughter. I heard you may also have another little one on the way. But, like I said, if you need anything…"

"Well, I do need a favor. Is it OK with you and Joe if Michelle spends the night there? I'll come by in the morning and take her to school."

"That won't be necessary. I'll take Michelle to school in the morning. You stay at home and get some rest. I'll call you tomorrow and see if you want me to keep her another night or just pick her up from school and bring her home."

"I appreciate all of your help, Edna. I'm gonna go and lie down for a while. I'll talk with you tomorrow."

"Goodnight, Sara."

I heard a loud sound while sitting in the living room. I peeped out the window. A black truck had just driven up in the driveway, playing loud country music. I quickly went into Michelle's room. She had a huge walk-in closet in her room that Mike built as a storage area for all of her toys. I went into the closet and hid there. I couldn't take anymore right then. I was tired and hurting, and all I wanted to do was get some rest.

Mike came into the house yelling, "Sara! Sara! Are you here! Damn that woman. She's not here. Come on in, Billy."

"Mike, we need to talk about the business. Profits are going down. The girls just ain't bringing in the crowds like they used to."

"Billy, you want a beer?"

"Yeah, make it a cold one. We're gonna have to think of something new."

"Billy, you're crazy. You said yourself that business ain't been this good since I came to this town. We got strippers, drugs, prostitutes, and female impersonators. Profits are gonna go up even more."

"But we've got to give the cops their cut just to keep the business going."

"You exaggerate too much, Billy. We've got this. Now get out of here so I can get some sleep."

Mike looked at his watch."Where in the hell is Sara?"

"Do you mean to tell me that you don't know where your wife is?"

"Her crazy family took her to the hospital."

"Is she sick?"

"No. I smacked her around a few times."

"Mike, you've got to stop that. You can't keep hitting on that girl. Why do you do that crap anyway? Look, I'm no saint. I'll admit, I've slapped Peggy around a few times when I had too much to drink. But trust me; I wouldn't hit her again for nothing in this world. When the cops came by to take me to jail, I resisted. Hell, I had been paying those guys off for years. I thought they were on my side. I soon learned my lesson. By the time they were finished with me, I had a broken arm and a broken collarbone. Man, they beat the hell out of me in that jail cell. I swore from that day on, I would never hit another woman again. Peggy is my heart and soul."

"I love Sara, but she drives me crazy sometimes. I just want to be free, you know, not tied down. I just want to be myself sometimes."

"Didn't you just say that she might be pregnant?"

"See! That's what I'm talking about. Another excuse to tie me down. I don't know…I've got to stop drinking. Yeah—things will get better if I stop drinking."

"I'm gonna get out of here so you can get some sleep, but, Mike, you better be careful. You can't keep hitting your wife. And don't forget, we need more money."

"Why are you complaining? We brought in at least ten thousand dollars last month."

"All right, man, I'm out of here. I'll see you tonight at work."

"Talk to you later, Billy."

I heard the front door close as I continued to sit in Michelle's closet.Trying not to make a sound, I eased the closet door closed. I heard Mike moving around in the kitchen, then

I heard footsteps in the hallway. It sounded like Mike closing the bedroom door, so I knew he had gone to bed.

I couldn't believe all the illegal things they had going on at that club. No wonder Mike could afford a new car. Those cops probably wouldn't have taken him to jail anyway, if they were being paid off. He acted as if he was concerned about where I was. I thought he did love us; he just seemed to be under a lot of pressure. It's his job that's stressing him out and tying him down, not me, I decided.

When I wondered what time it was, I realized I hadn't looked at my watch all day. The day seemed to go by so slowly. Everything was taking place in slow motion. My watch said it was about eight o'clock. My body felt so tired. I lay right there on the floor and went to sleep. I always loved the way the carpet felt on my skin.

I woke up later to a loud noise. No doubt it was Mike slamming the front door as usual. It was dark, so he must have been on his way to work. I got up from the floor slowly. I still felt pretty sore. When I walked over to Michelle's bedroom door, I saw headlights shining through the living room window. It was Mike backing out of the driveway leaving for work. My back still hurts, so I took a couple of Tylenol and got in the bed. I needed to get up early and try to make an appointment with my gynecologist.

Despite everything that happened, I had a good night's sleep. I was awakened by the sun shining in through the bedroom window. It was seven o'clock. I made myself hurry up. I had to get dressed and out of the house before Mike got there. I just couldn't face him right then. Part of me wanted to understand that he was stressed out because of his job and the drinking, but the other part of me couldn't forget that this man was willing to kick me in my stomach after I told him that I might be pregnant. Something about that entire thought just didn't feel right with me.

As much as it hurt, I got on my knees next to the bed and said a prayer. "Lord, protect me and my unborn child from danger and harm and give me the strength to continue to be a good mother and wife. Amen."

I quickly gathered my clothes and went into the bathroom for a shower. That warm water felt so good gliding over my body. It made me feel refreshed and ready to start a new day. Just the thought of carrying a new life inside of me gave me the courage to try to keep my family together. My stomach felt a little nauseous, so I planned to eat later. I did drink a glass of orange juice and ate a few crackers. I walked outside the front door and was greeted by beautiful bright sunshine. The air was so fresh, it reminded me of being back on the farm in the springtime. Abigail Peck was outside watering her garden.

"Good morning, Sara. A wonderful day that we're having."

"Good morning, Ms. Abigail," I replied as I rushed over to my car in the driveway. I got the feeling she thought I was interested in talking, but all I wanted to do was get over to Edna's house and spend some time with Michelle before driving her to school. I looked down the street, I didn't see Mike's car coming, so I quickly got into my car and drove away.

Traffic was pretty light for a Monday morning. I arrived at Edna's house just in time for breakfast. The smell of hot buttermilk biscuits and sweet hickory bacon danced in the air. I gently closed my eyes just for a moment to pretend I was back in Mama's kitchen at the farm. It felt so nice that it almost brought tears to my eyes.

"Sara, Sara, are you alright, child?"

"Oh, Edna. I'm fine. I was just reminiscing about the good old days."

Just then my cell phone rang. I was so deep in thought, the sound of my own cell phone darn near scared me to death. It was Mike. Should I answer or just let it ring? I knew if I didn't answer, he would probably keep calling me all day.

"Hello."

"Sara, where are you? I was worried about you, honey. You know I don't like for you to make me worry."

I had to stop that conversation before it went any further.

"I'm sorry, Mike. I just wanted to get an early start this morning. I'm gonna make an appointment with my gynecologist today. I'll make you some dinner when I get home this evening."

"Sara, I'm sorry. I think having another baby is a great idea. You know I get a little crazy when I drink too much. I love you, and I'd never do anything to hurt you."

"I know that you love me, and I love you too. Honey, I've got to go now. I've got to get Michelle off to school, and I don't like talking on my phone while I'm driving. I'll call you later."

"Talk to him while you're driving?" Uncle Joe asked when I hung up. "Sara, you're not driving."

"I just don't feel like to talking to him right now, Joe. Wow, I can't get over that wonderful smell of breakfast cooking in the kitchen."

"We were just about to sit down to breakfast. You're more than welcome to join us."

I couldn't resist. I had to sit down and eat something.

When breakfast was over, Joe went off to work and I took Michelle to school. Edna told me that I didn't have to work today. She told me to just hang around her house and try to get some rest. I made an appointment to see my gynecologist later on that day. I was still pretty tired from everything that had been going on, so I decided to take a nap. When I finally woke up, I had one hour to take a shower and get to my appointment. That sleep did me some good.

I couldn't stop rubbing my stomach. Just thinking about having a new life inside of me was fulfilling and warm. I couldn't wait to tell Michelle. She was going to be so excited.

CHAPTER FOURTEEN:

Pregnancy Confirmation

I went to see the gynecologist Dr. Susan Blake. Her bedside manner wasn't the world's best, but I liked her because she was strictly interested in her patients. I knew that she would give me the best care I could get for my baby. She even made house calls. Let's face it; there aren't too many doctors around, especially in the city, that make house calls. She confirmed that I was eight weeks pregnant. She gave me a prescription for prenatal vitamins and told me to watch my hemoglobin. Before, when I was pregnant with Michelle, I had problems with anemia. I told her I would try to improve my diet by adding iron-rich foods.

I could feel her eyes staring at my bruises during the examination. She didn't make any comments; she just told me to be careful and keep my monthly appointments. She gave me one of those smiles. You know the kind, the ones that are saying, *I'm not going to say anything, but I know how you really got those bruises*. On my way out the door, Dr. Blake walked up to me and handed me a bag. She smiled and walked away. When I got to the car, I looked inside the bag. It was filled with prenatal vitamins and iron pills. I also noticed at the bottom of the bag, there was a pamphlet: "If you are in trouble and you need someone to turn to, call this number, 1-800-DISEASE. Domestic violence. There is a cure for this disease."

I guess it was true what Joe said: everybody in the city of Henderson, Florida, did know that Mike was hitting me. Part of me wanted to go back into the office and tell her that she had accidentally put this pamphlet in my bag. But the other part of me was saying, go home Sara—just pretend it wasn't there.

It was getting late, and I wanted to get home to meet Michelle. As I drove along the street, I couldn't help but think, why did she have to let me know that she knew what was going on? Why did she have to put that damn pamphlet into my bag? I drove up into the driveway just in time. Edna was just dropping off Michelle. Mike's car was in the driveway also. I walked into the front door. They were all sitting in the living room.

"Hi, Mommy."

Michelle ran over to me and gave me a big hug and a kiss.

"Hello, Michelle. I missed you so much. Mommy loves you ,baby."

"I love you too, Mommy. I had fun at school today."

"Good. I'm so glad to hear that, and you can tell me all about it later at dinner, but now I want you to go into your room and change your clothes."

"Yes, ma'am."

"Go ahead and start your homework and I'll go over it with you."

"Yes, Mommy."

"I love you."

"I love you too, Mommy." Michelle went running into her bedroom.

"So, how are you feeling?" Edna asked with a huge smile on her face.

"I feel pretty good. My doctor confirmed that I was eight weeks pregnant and so far, everything is just fine with the baby."

Mike walked over and stood in front of me. I was thinking to myself, I know he's not going to try and hit me in front of Edna. He put his arms around my waist and began to hug me. He looked me straight in the eyes and said, "Sara, I am so sorry for all of the hell that I've put you through over the years. Please forgive me."

Oh my goodness, he just meant what he said. "It's alright, Mike. I know that you've been under a lot of stress, and I am so sorry for making you feel that way. I just want us to be happy. That's all I've ever wanted all of my life."

We both stood in the middle of the living room embracing each other with tears in our eyes. Edna also put her arms around the both of us.

"I've got to get home and start dinner for Joe. Are you two gonna be alright?"

"We're fine, Aunt Edna," Mike replied. I smiled at her with tears of joy in my eyes. For the first time in a long time, I felt like things were going to be alright with Mike and me.

"I'll see you at work tomorrow, Edna."

"No Sara, just take the rest of the week off and get some rest."

"I love you, Edna, and thank you for everything. I do appreciate all of your help."

She kissed me gently on the forehead and just smiled at me as she walked out of the front door. I wiped the tears from my eyes. "Well, I guess I better fix some dinner."

"No, you don't have to fix dinner. I went out and got some food from the club. I've got cheeseburgers, pizza, French fries, and sodas. I just want you to take it easy. Besides, you're gonna be a mother again and I'm gonna be a father again. Why don't we both tell Michelle the good news over dinner?"

"That sounds like a good idea. She's always saying that she wished she had a little brother or a little sister to play with."

Mike and I kissed each other passionately. "Maybe if it's a little boy, then we can name him Michael Jr."

"That sounds like a good idea."

We both walked into the kitchen. "Michelle, honey, it's time for dinner." I said.

Michelle came into the kitchen, and we all sat down at the table for dinner.

Later that night, Mike wanted to make love, but we both were too tired and too sore. All we could do was just kiss each other good night as we fell asleep in each other's arms. Mike woke up about ten that night and left for work. I immediately fell back to sleep.

I must admit, things were pretty good for a while. I went back to work at the shop. Business had picked up. Edna and I decided to take a chance and increase our clothing line. We went from just selling dresses to selling just about everything a woman could wear. We sold shirts, pants, lingerie, hair products, makeup, purses and accessories, jewelry, shoes, anything a woman could buy to give herself a complete makeover. We even added a maternity section in the back of the store. Everything an expecting mother could want for her baby. Profits were good.

I was so proud of the shop. Edna and I put a lot of time and effort into making the business a big success. Mike was still going to work every night. He increased his hours; at least that's what he told me. He was gone from the house more than ever. He only came home to shower and take a nap. Some days he didn't come home at all. I missed him, but I couldn't help but enjoy the time that he wasn't at the house. When Mike was at home, I felt like I was walking on eggs, trying hard not to break any of them. I hated that feeling.

I did notice that the phone would ring every night, but when I answered it, the person on the other end would hang up. The caller ID just said "Private Name." One night Mike answered the phone. I guess he didn't realize or even notice that I was standing next to the bedroom door in the hallway. "Hello. Damn it, I told you not to call me on this phone."

Mike closed the bedroom door. I was so tempted to pick up the other phone in the kitchen, but I knew if Mike found out, he would probably kill me. It was the same person who had been calling the house every night at this time. The caller ID said "Private Name." He soon came out of the bedroom back into the kitchen. He looked at me and smiled. "That was just the wrong number."

"Yeah, it seems as if the wrong number has been calling here a lot lately."

Mike just started laughing. "Yeah, we do get a lot of wrong numbers. So, what's for dinner, honey?" I didn't know what he was up to, but I had a feeling that nothing good would come of it. We all sat down at the table for dinner.

CHAPTER FIFTEEN:

Tom's Heart Attack

I was about five months pregnant now. I hadn't seen Mama in about three months. I wanted to call and talk to her, but I really wanted to go and visit. The last time I called her house, Janie answered the phone. I tried to make conversation, but all she did was say, "I'll go get Mama for you," and she put down the phone. I was afraid she hated me. I felt that maybe if we could just talk face to face, somehow she could find it in her heart to forgive me. I just wished I could close my eyes and allow time to turn itself back. I think I would have done things a lot differently. For the first time in all these years, I finally admitted to myself that if I had the chance again, I don't think I would have married Mike Farraday. I decided to call Mama and tell her that Michelle and I would come by and visit the farm that weekend.

"Mama. This is Sara."

Mama sounded tired. "Hello, Sara."

"Are you alright? You sound so tired."

"Well, I am a little tired. I've been spending some nights at the hospital with Tom. He seems to be getting better. He'll probably be discharged home in a couple of days."

"Wait a minute. What's wrong with Mr. Farraday?"

"Mike didn't tell you?"

"Tell me what, Mama?"

"Tom had a heart attack. It was only a mild one, thank goodness, but he's gonna have to take it easy."

"Do Edna and Joe know what happened?"

"They're driving down today after work to spend the weekend."

" I wonder why she didn't mention anything to me."

"Well, she spoke with Mike. He knows that his father had a heart attack. As a matter of fact, he drove up here this morning."

"You've got to be kidding, Mama. How could he not tell me that his own father had a heart attack and he was going to see him?"

"No, honey, I said that he drove up here this morning, I didn't say anything about him going to visit his father."

"Mama, he hasn't been by the hospital?"

"Not yet. Timmy saw him in town earlier today. He assumed you were with him. Timmy said he went up to Mike's car and he saw a lady with red hair sitting on the passenger side. Mike didn't even speak to him. He acted as if he didn't know who Timmy was. Sara, how have you been doing?"

"I'm doing fine Mama. I was calling to see if it was OK with you if Michelle and I came to the farm this weekend for a visit, but if Mike is hanging around Loxley, then maybe we should wait for some other time."

"No! You bring my granddaughter here for a visit. Mike won't set foot out here on this farm, especially if he's parading some other woman in town. Plus, this will give you and your sister some time to talk. That argument that the two of you had is still bothering her. You know she'd never admit it, but I know that Janie still loves you."

"I miss talking to her too, Mama."

"I'm gonna go back to the hospital and check on Tom."

"Mama, you know the two of you should get married."

"I thought about it, but I think it's best for the both of us if we just continue to be good friends. Don't misunderstand, I do care a lot about Tom and I know that he cares a lot about me as well. You see, Tom really loved his first wife, and it nearly destroyed him when she died. He held his own son responsible for her death for several years. I know I can never take the place of Elizabeth Farraday in his soul, so I'll just be Julia Ramsey in his heart. Now, you go and get my granddaughter all packed up, and I will see you both on tomorrow. I love you, Sara."

"I love you too, Mama. See you tomorrow."

I couldn't believe that Mike went to Loxley without even telling me, but I wasn't surprised. He wasn't at home half the time to tell me anything. I just wished Edna or Joe would have called. I guess they thought that wonderful nephew of theirs would have had the decency to at least tell me that his father was in the hospital. I started to get our things together for the trip in the morning.

Saturday morning came pretty fast. I tossed and turned all night. My mind was still on poor Mr. Farraday. I hoped that he got better soon. He wasn't much on personality, but he was a good man. I wondered if he had spent more time as a father to Mike, would Mike have turned out to be a different person. I was still upset with Mike for not telling me what was going on. Did he hate me? I thought if he hated me, he'd ask me for a divorce. OK, Sara, I told myself, enough of that this morning. Time to get up out of bed and get the ball rolling.

I thought I'd take a shower and get dressed before starting breakfast. My stomach felt pretty queasy. I thought I'd just fix Michelle a bowl of cereal and I would just have some toast. My stomach was getting so big. I couldn't wait to have the baby. The ultrasound had said that it was a boy. I hoped that Mike will calm down and spend some time with Michael Jr. He needed to spend more time with Michelle as well. When I was a little girl, I would have loved it if my father had stayed with us instead of leaving. I missed not having him in my life as a child. I don't want Michelle growing up feeling that way. Tired of thinking, I hit the shower.

What a beautiful day it was. The birds were singing and the sky was baby blue with huge white clouds. I walked into

Michelle's room expecting to find her still asleep, but she was wide awake watching cartoons.

"Mommy, Mommy, I'm ready to go to the farm. When are we going to leave?"

"Well, good morning to you too, sweetie. First, you have to wash your face and hands."

"I already did that, Mommy. Can I get dressed now so that we can leave? I want to get there in time to ride the ponies."

"You have to eat breakfast first. I'm gonna fix you a bowl of cereal and you can have a glass of orange juice, then we'll both get dressed and hit the road."

"Mommy, is Daddy coming with us?"

"No, baby, he's not coming with us. It's just you and me, kid. Oh, and don't forget Michael Jr."

"Mommy, why come Daddy never goes anywhere with us?"

"Honey, Daddy works a lot."

"My friend Monica said that her daddy takes her to the movies and to the zoo. Daddy never takes me anywhere. He won't even play with me. Mommy, did I do something to make Daddy mad? I love him, but I don't think he loves me."

Oh my goodness. I fought so hard to keep from crying in front of Michelle. What should I say? What could I say to my little girl to make her believe that her daddy loved her? What lies can I tell this time?

"Sweetie, Daddy is going to meet us in Loxley."

"He is?"

"Yes, he is. Grandma Julia said that Daddy was already there. Grandpa Tom is in the hospital and Daddy had to go and visit him."

"What's wrong with Grandpa?"

"He got sick. His heart felt bad, so he had to go to the hospital."

"Did he have to get a shot from the nurse, like I did when I was sick?"

"Yes, he had to get a shot, but he had to stay at the hospital so the doctor could make sure that the shot worked. We'll go by the hospital and visit with him. Would you like to do that?"

"Yes, Mommy. Can we take him some balloons with the smiley faces on them?"

"I bet Grandpa would like that. Now, let's go and eat breakfast so we can hit the road."

That worked out just fine at the time, but I didn't know what I was going to say the next time she asked me if her daddy loves her.

It didn't take long to pack up the car and get to Loxley. Michelle was so tired, she slept the entire trip. They had paved the road leading to the house. I remembered many days when Timmy and I walked home from school on that dirt road. Things had changed. Everything looked so different. The city had even provided more streetlights.

"Wake up, Michelle."

"Are we here, Mommy?"

"Yes, honey. Grab your backpack, while I undo your seatbelt."

Everyone came outside when we drove up, except Janie. "Hello, everybody. Hi, Mama."

"Hello, Sara. Come in and make yourself right at home. I'm going to Tom's house. Edna just called and said that he has been discharged from the hospital. I'm going to his house and make sure everything is ready for his arrival. I'll be back later. There's plenty of food in the refrigerator. Oh, let me give my grandbaby a big hug. I love you, Michelle. I'll be back in a few hours. Timmy, help your sister with her bags."

Mama rushed off quickly. She was so crazy about Tom Farraday. I just wished the two of them could admit to themselves how much they cared about each other.

"Timmy, you are so tall. Oh, my goodness, you have a mustache?"

"Hello to you too, sis. Yes, I have a mustache. My fiancée likes it."

"Are you engaged?"

"Sara, I called your house a couple of months ago. I talked to Mike. He said that he would give you the message that I'm getting married in December. I just figured you were busy working or just tired and you'd call me back one day."

"Mike never gave me the message."

"Well, I told you years ago, that guy was a real live creep. I saw him yesterday in town. I thought the two of you were here together, but I see that it wasn't you that he was parading up and down the streets with. I thought about driving to Florida a few times to talk to him about the way he's been treating you. I don't like the things that I'm hearing about your relationship with Mike."

"Timmy, I don't want you to worry about me. I want to hear more about your wedding plans later. I have missed you guys so much. I love you all. You all mean the world to me and Michelle."

"I love you too, Sara."

"Hi, Rex."

"Hey, Sara. Come over here and give me a hug girl. We have missed you and Michelle around here. Speaking of Michelle, there's my pretty little angel. Are you ready to go for a ride? We just got in two new ponies a couple of weeks ago. I think you'll like them."

"Mommy, can I go riding with Uncle Rex? I want to see the new ponies."

"That will give you a chance to talk to Janie. She tried to call you twice, but Mike answered the phone. She did leave a message with him once to tell you to call her."

"Damn that Mike. He never gave me any messages from any of my family. I am so pissed off with him right now. You mean Janie wants to talk to me?"

"Yes," Rex replied. "Go up to the main house. She's doing some advertisements for her mother. Come on, little one. Let's go riding."

Rex grabbed Michelle and put her on his back as he went galloping down to the stables pretending to be a horse. Rex was a good man. Apparently, he was the closest person to a father that Michelle would ever have in her life. I immediately headed for the main house. I opened the door and stopped dead in my tracks. Oh my goodness, what could I say to my sister? Mike, that bastard, he didn't give me any of the messages that they left. I knew she probably thought that I was a real live monster.

I slowly walked into the living room, afraid that I might say the wrong things and lose the love of my sister forever. The person who had protected me from harm since I was a little girl. My words had to be chosen carefully. I walked down the hallway into the den. There sat Janie, working hard as usual. She didn't notice that I had entered the room.

"Janie."

I called her name as tears began to roll down my face. I couldn't hold them back any longer. I had missed my big sister. She immediately jumped up from her desk and ran over to me.

"Sara, are you alright?" She wrapped her arms around me and gave me a big hug. It felt so good.

"I'm fine, Janie, now that I'm here with you all. I've missed you so much. I am so sorry. Mike didn't give me any of the messages that you all left for me. I had no idea that you had called. We need to talk. Can you ever forgive me for what I said that day at the house? Janie, I have always loved you and I always will. Mike is just my husband, but you are my blood."

Both of us stood there hugging each other with tears in our eyes. Janie finally forgave me. I felt so complete having my sister back into my life.

We all had lunch together about midday. I had missed eating those fresh vegetables that Mama grew in the garden. Everything tasted so good. Michelle was having a good time. Janie and I talked after lunch. She said that she and Rex were getting married in the winter, along with Jimmy and his fiancée. Jimmy worked as a chemical engineering assistant at the paper mill. He was scheduled to take his exam for his license in two weeks. My little brother was going to be a licensed chemical engineer.

Janie and Rex had completely renovated their entire house. It was so beautiful. I couldn't stop crying. I was so excited for everyone. I told her that the baby was due in four months. His name was Michael Jr.

"We'll probably call him MJ for short," I said.

Janie finally asked me the question that I had been trying to avoid. "Sara, where is Mike? Timmy said that he saw him yesterday."

I had to think of something fast and convincing. Janie could always look into my eyes and tell if I was lying. "He's at the hospital with his dad."

"Well, that's strange. Mama has been going by to see Mr. Farraday every day, and she didn't mention Mike being there."

"He called me early this morning and said that he was on his way to the hospital."

Janie just looked at me and smiled. "Same old Mike. Sara, it's alright. You're talking to your sister, not just some woman who doesn't know any better. I'm sure Mike probably hasn't seen his dad since he's been in Loxley. Now, tell me how you've been doing, and please tell me the truth."

I swear Janie had to have a sixth sense about people telling lies.

"I'm alright. I have my good days and my bad days. Most of all right now, I just want to give birth to a healthy son. The shop is doing great. Edna and I have expanded our clothing line. As you can see, Michelle is just growing like a weed. She is so smart. She'll start first grade in the fall."

Janie looked me straight in the eyes and asked me point-blank, "When is the last time that Mike hit you?"

I couldn't say a word. I sat there as if I were a store mannequin. My lips wouldn't move. What did she want me to say... Yes, Mike was still hitting me at least every two or three weeks. I said nothing.

"Sara...I shouldn't have asked you that. I apologize. Just never forget as long as you live, if you ever need somewhere to go, just call Mama or myself and we will help you at any time. I love you, Sara Ann Ramsey, and you will always be Sara Ann Ramsey to me."

Janie held my hands, and with tears in her eyes, she kissed me gently on my forehead.

Beep. Beep. Beep. "Who's blowing their car horn?" Janie asked. We both rushed over to the den window. "Mama?"

It was Mama, but she wasn't alone. Low and behold, she had the great Tom Farraday sitting on the passenger side.

"Sara, let's go outside and see what's going on."

"I agree, Janie."

We went outside. Rex and two of the other ranch hands brought some suitcases from the car into the house. Mama got out of the car with a smile on her face. She walked over to the passenger side and opened the door for Tom.

"Everybody, Tom is going to be staying in the guest room for a while. The doctors didn't want him going home alone, so I thought it would be a great idea for him to stay here with us."

Janie looked at me and I looked at her. We both just started smiling and went over to greet Mr. Farraday. Mama walked next to Tom with her arm around his waist. She helped him inside the house. They looked absolutely wonderful together. I think for the first time in years, Tom Farraday had a smile on his face. We all helped Tom to get situated in the guest room. He talked and attempted to play with Michelle for at least two hours. He had missed her. He did mention that he hadn't heard from Mike in almost three years, except for one day he came to Loxley to try to borrow some money.

"Mike came down to Loxley and asked me for a loan for five thousand dollars. I asked him what he needed the money for. Mike got upset with me and said that he needed it for a business investment. I told him I couldn't loan him that kind of money if he didn't have a legitimate reason for borrowing it. Edna's been keeping me informed of Mike's behavior. Billy's father would roll over in his grave if he knew what kind of business that boy has been running with the money that he left him. I haven't heard from Mike since that day. Sara, I would like to apologize for Mike's behavior. I should have raised that boy better than I did. I take full responsibility for his actions."

"Mr. Farraday, it's not your fault. Mike's just been under a lot of stress. He's been trying to make a lot of money for the family, and it just gets to be a little too much for him sometimes. Please don't blame yourself. Things are much better, now that I'm pregnant with your grandson. Mike has changed."

Who are you trying to fool, Sara, I thought. These people don't believe a word that you are saying.

"OK, everybody, it's been a long day and it's getting late. Why don't we let Tom get some rest?"

"That sounds like a good idea, Mama," Janie said. "Why don't we all call it a night?"

Michelle was so tired, Timmy had to carry her upstairs. Rex and Janie walked down behind the barn to their house. Mama spent the night downstairs next to the guest room where Tom was sleeping, just in case he needed anything in the middle of the night. I must admit, those two looked like a real couple. I finally went upstairs. I was almost dreading the fact that I had to drive back to the real world the next day. There was so much love and warmth here. I wished Mike and I could have that feeling in our home and in our hearts. I was going to talk to him as soon as I got home. I wanted to know why he didn't take just a small amount of time out of his busy schedule to visit his father in the hospital. As a matter of fact, we had a lot of talking to do, but first I needed to get some rest. I was sure gonna miss this place. I hated saying goodbye.

The rooster was crowing the next morning. It was a familiar sound. I called it nature's alarm clock. We all had breakfast together. Mama was smiling and blushing at Tom Farraday. He returned her smile with a wink of the eye. The doctors said that he would be fine this time, but he had to be careful of any excessive amounts of stress. I had a feeling that he would be hanging around the house for a while, especially if Mama got her way about the subject.

Next came the time that I regretted, saying goodbye to everyone. Michelle started to cry because she didn't want to leave, but I promised her that as soon as the baby was born, we would drive up and stay for a week. She was happy about that idea. We headed out for our trip back. I was surprised at Janie and Mama—no advice, just a kiss and a hug this time.

CHAPTER SIXTEEN:

Mike's Erratic Behavior

Our two-hour drive turned out to be a three-hour drive. I wanted to think about what I was going to say to Mike when I got home. I wanted to make sure that I chose each word carefully; I wasn't in the mood to drag myself up from the floor today. I wondered if I should wait until he was in a good mood. What was I saying? The man was probably not at home. He was probably still running around town with that bitch back in Loxley. Oh well, we were finally home.

"Michelle, honey, we're here." Michelle always fell asleep when we went for long drives. We got everything into the house just as the phone started to ring.

"Hello. Hi, Edna. How are you and Joe doing? Why didn't you tell me that your brother was in the hospital? I'm glad to hear that Tom was alright and that it was just a false alarm. He's gonna have to be a little more careful with his diet and his stress. Mama is enjoying him being at the house. She'll probably spoil him so much, he may never leave. When did you and Joe get back in town? Oh, the two of you got home just before Michelle and I did. No, I didn't see Mike and I haven't heard from him either, but I'm pretty sure that he's alright. If he doesn't show up for dinner, then I'll give him a call. I promise that I won't provoke him. Well, I'm gonna get things situated and I'll see you tomorrow at work. Give Joe my love. Talk to you later. Goodbye, Edna."

Just as I was getting Michelle ready for her bath, I heard Mike's car drive up. He came into the house singing as if everything was just fine. "Michelle, honey, you stay in your room and watch cartoons. I'm gonna talk with your daddy for a little while."

"Alright, Mommy."

I walked out of Michelle's room and closed the door. The liquor on Mike's breath was so strong, I could smell it before I even got close to him.

"Hi, Sara. What's going on?" He started to laugh as if something was really funny.

"Where have you been, Mike? I thought that you were in Loxley to see your father. You do know that he's been in the hospital, don't you?"

"I know that he's been in the hospital. Don't raise your voice at me, Sara. Ain't nothing wrong with that old man. He'll probably outlive all of us. With all the hate he has in his heart for me, I think I'm the last person that he wants to visit him."

"Well, if you didn't go to Loxley to visit with your dad, why did you go there?"

"Who told you that I went to Loxley? Oh...I remember now. It was that nosy-ass brother of yours. What is he doing? Is he spying for you, or do you have some detectives following me around?"

He kept walking closer and closer to me. I noticed that his eyes were red and his speech was a little slurred. I slowly began to back away. I knew I couldn't talk to him when he was drunk. My words were limited as I just kept smiling.

"Why are you smiling?" he asked. "Is there something funny? Well, don't keep it to yourself, tell me about it. I want to smile and laugh too."

Mike started to laugh loud like some kind of nutcase. I decided I better change the subject altogether. "It's OK, Mike. We're both home, so why don't I cook something to eat. I don't know about you, but I'm getting a little hungry. Michelle is probably hungry also. I know, we can all have tuna salad. It will only take a few minutes to fix."

I turned around to walk toward the kitchen door, when suddenly Mike grabbed my arm. "Where do you think you're going? You don't walk away from me when I'm talking to you." Mike grabbed my upper arms and started shaking me.

"Mike…Honey, it's alright."

He slapped me across my face. "You don't tell me where to go or what to do! Do you understand?"

Oh, my fingers. He grabbed my hand and squeezed it so hard. It felt as if my fingers were breaking, one by one. My mind kept telling me to push him away, but I knew if I tried anything, he would probably beat me or even kill me. He slapped me again. I screamed out in pain; I tried not to, but I couldn't keep it inside anymore. My face hurt so bad. By that time, I heard Michelle screaming.

"Mommy! Are you alright?" I could tell by her voice that she was crying. "Daddy, please don't hit Mommy? Please, Daddy!"

Mike began to mock Michelle, speaking as if he were a child. "Daddy, don't hit Mommy, please, Daddy, please…Oh, forget this crap."

He pushed me down onto the sofa. "I'm out of here."

He turned around, picked up his keys, and walked out the front door, slamming it behind him. Michelle ran over to the sofa and gave me a big hug. She was so afraid. I hated to see my little girl crying. I heard Mike's car driving off down the street.

"Mommy, your face is so red."

It was burning. I looked like I had been sitting in the sun all day. From that moment, I realized that Mike had fallen victim to some kind of mental disease—domestic violence. I continued to hug Michelle.

"Sweetie, it's gonna be alright. Mommy's face hurts a little, but I'm gonna be just fine."

"Why does Daddy hurt you like that, Mommy?"

"Michelle, Daddy's sick. He's under a lot pressure and stress. He doesn't mean to hurt Mommy. I'm hoping that one day he will go to the doctor and get some help for his problem."

"Is he gonna hit me too, Mommy?"

"No, baby. I'll never let him touch you."

I was in a lot of pain, but I managed to get myself together for the sake of my daughter and my unborn son.

"Come on, Michelle, it's time for dinner.

Michelle finally calmed down after her bath. I gave her a kiss on the cheek and tucked her into bed for the night. My face was still burning. I applied an ice pack for a few minutes to help ease the burning sensation. I was so tired of Mike's erratic behavior. He was almost out of control. I wanted to find out why he was really in Loxley. Maybe he had intentions of seeing his dad and decided not to at the last minute.

I put the ice pack aside. The baby was kicking a lot. I hoped he wasn't taking after his father. Mike was gone, and I hoped he wouldn't be back that night. I needed a good night's sleep. I was so tired; I didn't worry about taking a shower. I changed my clothes and got into bed under the covers.

The bed felt so good. My hand hurt, but at least I knew it wasn't broken. I was so tired that I fell asleep before my head hit the pillow. I knew I had been sleeping for a while, when all of a sudden, I felt a strange feeling. It was as if all the life was being drained out of my body. It felt like a noose being tightened around my neck. What was going on? When I finally managed to open my eyes, Mike was straddling my body with his hands around my neck, choking the life out of me. What was he doing? Was he trying to kill me? I couldn't breathe. My hands attempted to scratch his face, but I couldn't. There was no more fight left inside of me. Just as I was slowly closing my eyes, I said a prayer to myself: "Lord, don't let it end like this. Please don't take me from my children."

All of a sudden, Mike let go of my neck. He began to laugh. I could smell the stench of stale beer on his breath. I grabbed my neck and tried desperately to catch my breath. He continued to laugh so hard that he fell out of bed onto the floor. That bastard was crazy. I got out of bed and stood up, continuing to try and catch my breath.

"I'm sorry, Sara," Mike said as he continued to laugh hysterically. "I'm not trying to kill you. I was only kidding around." I ran out of the room. "Sara...Don't act like that. I said I was joking with you."

I ran into the living room. There, sitting on the sofa, was the tall blond-headed man. Mike's new friend. He also was laughing as if it were all some sort of sick joke. I ran into Michelle's room and locked the door. She had slept through all the noise. Mike came to the door, screaming, "Sara! You're too sensitive, baby! It must be your hormones. I love you, baby."

He was laughing with each word that he spoke. "Come on, man, let's get out of here. Sara's in a cranky mood tonight."

The front door shut. A few minutes later, I heard Mike's car backing out of the driveway. It was eleven thirty at night. Why did he come home, and who was that guy in the living room? His face looked familiar for some reason. I put a chair behind Michelle's door just in case those two came back. I couldn't help but cry. I had never been that scared before in my life. I lay down next to Michelle and finally dozed off to sleep.

Morning came pretty fast. With all my tossing and turning, I may have gotten about two hours of sleep. Time to rise and shine. Michelle was still sleeping. She could probably sleep through a bomb exploding. She inherited that from her father. My face was still red. If anybody asked what happened, I would tell them that I got sunburn. My neck was bruised.

Standing there looking in the mirror, there was a woman staring back at me. Who was she? Someone who had become a victim in her own home. Suffering from a disease known only as domestic violence. Lying, being manipulated by a man that I thought was my true love. I was ashamed to look at myself. Who was this stranger trying to hide her bruises, putting on a smile pretending that everything was just fine, and lying to my daughter? What kind of a mother was I? Mama would have never taken this kind of treatment from a man. I was too embarrassed and ashamed to even tell her or anyone else just what I was going through.

Come on, Sara, let's get with the program, I told myself. I decided to wear my button-down white silk shirt. Along with a little extra makeup, no one should notice any of the bruises.

After taking my shower and getting dressed for work, I prepared breakfast. "Come on, Michelle, it's time to eat."

I had to get a move on things so we could get out of there on time. It was another crazy Monday morning. Everybody was in a hurry, including me. I dropped Michelle off at school; at least half of the task was over. As I pulled into the back parking lot of the employee entrance, I glanced at my watch. Darn, late again. I snuck into the basement door. Good, nobody down there.

As I walked by trying to make as little noise as possible, I noticed several boxes of silk scarfs. No one would mind if I borrow the lovely green one, I thought. Besides, it matched my hunter green pants. It would hide the bruises on my neck.

Just as I was walking up the stairs to my office, I ran into Lisa. Business was expanding so fast that Edna had to hire four other ladies to help run the store. Lisa was young and nosy. Always asking me stupid questions. How did you get that bruise? Where did those scratches come from? Sara, you look pale today, aren't you getting enough sleep? She got on my nerves. But I must admit, she was a good bookkeeper and sales representative. She could sell ice to an Eskimo, and her good looks and long legs helped her to get her master's degree at such a young age.

"Hi, Sara. We were wondering where you were. Please... Tell me that you haven't assigned inventory duties to anyone. Shannon and I were interested in the overtime. I was going to ask Edna, but she told me to get with you about the inventory schedule. Shannon and I could stay over a few nights next week and take care of the new shipments."

"There are a lot of boxes down here, Lisa. I kind of figured it would take at least five people to take care of this shipment. Are you sure that you and Shannon can handle this entire inventory by yourselves?"

"Yes, ma'am. Shannon just broke up with her boyfriend, so we decided to get an apartment together. The only problem is that the manager wants first and last month's rent, along with a security deposit and an application fee. But it's worth it. The apartments are located downtown, not too far from here."

"How is Shannon doing? Edna said that she called in sick for the week. Is she feeling any better?"

"Shannon wasn't sick. She broke up with her boyfriend. I'm telling you this because I trust you and I know you won't mention this conversation to anyone. Shannon went to her boyfriend's family reunion about two weeks ago. She didn't want to go, but Brad talked her into going with him. Brad wandered off for a few minutes, so Shannon went to look for him. She walked around thirty-five acres of land at his grandmother's house. When she went inside the house and went upstairs, she caught Brad having sex with his sister's thirteen-year-old daughter. Shannon said that the girl wasn't putting up a fight, so evidently this wasn't the first time."

"Oh my goodness, Lisa. I feel so sorry for Shannon. Just the thought of incest makes me sick to my stomach. Doesn't Shannon have a little girl?"

"Yes. She has a seven-year-old named Taylor. Shannon asked her if Brad ever touched her inappropriately. She told her no. I'm so glad that she dumped that guy. Do you know that there are probably some women out there who would have held onto that sick jerk even after seeing him having sex with his own niece? Some women feel that if they don't have a man in their lives, they don't feel complete. A man makes them feel like a whole person."

I was getting a little tired of Lisa rambling on and on. "You know, Sara, I know that a lot of people think that I don't like men, just because I'm not in a relationship. But the fact of the matter is, I refuse to let a man treat me like dirt. I am twenty-two years old with a master's degree in accounting and bookkeeping. I can take care of myself. I am a whole person and until the right man comes along, I will continue to be single."

Trying desperately to change the subject, I said, "I'll go ahead and schedule you and Shannon for the inventory. I'm glad she's feeling better. Well, I better get back to work. Monday is a busy day in the business world."

"Thank you. I appreciate the overtime. Sara…That scarf you're wearing looks familiar. It goes great with your outfit, but isn't it a little too warm today for a button-down silk blouse and a silk scarf?"

Nosy, nosy, nosy, I mumbled under my breath. "Lisa, when you're in the fashion business, you have to be a walking mannequin for advertisement. If people don't see it, how can they buy it?"

"That's a great idea. I'll put out some of the scarfs today on the accessories table. Yeah…Scarfs are also good for hiding things too. Don't you think so, Sara? I better get to work. Talk with you later. Thanks again for the overtime, boss."

Lisa jogged up the stairs in her three-inch stilettos. She made me sick. I was sure some of those comments she made were aimed at me. When it came down to personality, she was a real live piece of work, or should I say, a real live bitch. But she was good at her job. I had heard some of the ladies gossiping about her being a lesbian. Maybe she was just a smart woman when it came down to men. I could recall a conversation I overheard. She told Edna that women had a better chance of winning the lottery than finding a good man. I wondered.

Time was flying by, so I needed to get to work. I wasn't in the mood for anymore conversations at this time. I thought I would stay down in the basement and check out the old and the new merchandise shipments from last week. That way, I wouldn't have to run into Lisa again.

Where had the time gone? It was almost four thirty. I couldn't believe I had been working down there for eight hours. It was time to wrap things up for the day, so I could go pick up Michelle from school. I wasn't in the cooking mood, so we could order pizza. Michelle loved pizza. I could hear her little voice saying, "Mommy, please order the one with all of the different kinds of meat.

Mike Farraday. Would he be at home, or where would he be? Right then, I could care less. I just hoped he was acting more normal than yesterday. He was a nice man, but when he got stressed out and started drinking, he went from Dr. Jekyll to Mr. Hyde.

"Sara. Sara, are you still here?" Edna called out.

"I was just about to lock up down here, Edna, and leave for the day."

"Don't worry about that. I'll lock up everything. I've still got some last-minute things to do. You just get out of here and go pick up Michelle. It's getting late. I'll see you tomorrow."

"Goodnight, Edna."

As I got into my car and drove out of the parking lot, I realized just how tired I was. It took all of my energy trying to work and avoid as many employees all day as possible. I couldn't deal with anymore questions about my scarf and my shirt. Lisa had already worn me out from the morning's conversations.

The traffic was hectic that evening. It was a beautiful day, I had to admit. I loved the outdoors. The sun was playing peekaboo in between the huge white clouds, with a baby blue sky in the background. I liked driving with the windows down. There was a smell of fresh-cut grass in the air. I guess that's what happens when you grow up on a farm.

As I drove up into the school parking lot, I saw Michelle's teacher, along with some of her other teachers, standing out front. I looked at the children, but I didn't see Michelle. Slowly driving up to the curve, I continued to look around the schoolyard. Not a glimpse of her anywhere. Tonya, Michelle's teacher, noticed my car parked alongside the curve.

"Hello, Sara. What are you doing here?"

"I came to pick up Michelle."

"Your husband picked up Michelle a couple of hours ago."

"Tonya, are you serious?"

"Yes...Mike said he wanted to pick her up early today and spend some time with her. Did I do something wrong by letting her go with him?"

"No. You know what? It's my fault. I forgot that Mike said he was going to pick Michelle up today. I'm really sorry. I'll see you tomorrow."

I drove off calmly, but in my head I was wondering why in the hell he would pick up Michelle without telling me first. He had never picked her up from school before. Damn him. What was he up to? I knew he wouldn't hurt his own child. The speedometer was up to eighty. I hoped there were no police around. I couldn't reach him on his cell phone. I couldn't even remember if it was the right number.

"Come on, people, get out of the way!" Everyone wanted to drive so slow. I had to get home. Why was I crying? He wouldn't hurt her, or would he? My hands wouldn't stop shaking.

When I got home, Mike's car was there. I drove up into the driveway, jumped out of the car, and ran toward the house in a panic. I didn't know what I would find inside. All I could do was pray that my daughter was safe. I glanced over at the two sisters sitting on their front porch. Sorry, ladies, but I didn't have time to deal with the two of them. I ran up the steps and slung open the front door.

"Surprise!" There stood Mike and Michelle in the living room waiting for me to get home. "Happy Birthday, Mommy!"

"Happy birthday, Sara!" There was a birthday cake on the table, along with two pizza boxes. So much had been going on the last few days, I had forgotten that today was my birthday.

"Mommy, why are you crying? You've got makeup all over your shirt, Mommy."

I was so glad to see Michelle. All I could do was put my arms around her.

"What's wrong, Mommy?"

"I was scared when I got to the school and Tonya told me that you were gone."

"Daddy came by to pick me up early so we could have a birthday party for you."

"I'm sorry, Sara. I just wanted to surprise you. Didn't Tonya tell you that I picked up Michelle early?"

"Yes, she did. But you have never picked up Michelle before. I thought something was wrong." I was so overwhelmed that I couldn't stop crying.

"Sara, honey, why don't you go and get cleaned up, and then we'll have some pizza before it gets cold."

I walked by the mirror in the hallway. Oh my goodness, my face looked a mess.

"I will go and wash my face. I better change my clothes as well. Why don't the two of you set the table and I'll be right back in a couple of minutes."

"OK, Sara. Hurry up. I'm ready to eat," Mike replied. It didn't take me long to wash the makeup and the tears from my face. Mike harming Michelle. No...I don't think he would ever go that far.

My silk blouse was probably ruined. My tears had washed the majority of my makeup onto my shirt. The cleaners were gonna have a task ahead of them trying to get those stains out. The pajama top I slipped on was nice and comfortable. Well, off to my birthday party, I thought. My body was almost numb from the panic I had just experienced.

Somehow I managed to force myself to attend my birthday party, to make my little girl happy. Mike and Michelle were already sitting down at the table eating pizza and drinking sodas.

"Hey, you guys, save some for me."

I sat down between the two of them. This was good. For the first time in a long time, I felt we were a family.

CHAPTER SEVENTEEN:

The Next Four Months

Things were pretty good for the next four months. The store continued to blossom from a plant to a beautiful tree. Edna was so proud. Everyone was surprised that a few women could change a small dress shop into a downtown clothing store. Mike was in and out of the house. He worked seven days a week. He spent more and more time at the club. We stopped having sex. Mike hadn't touched me in about four months now. The warmth and companionship of a good man—sounds so simple, but yet it remains the hardest task in a woman's life.

I had my weekends off. Janie, Mama, and I took Michelle to Disney World for her birthday. Tom Farraday pretty much paid for the trip, but he wasn't able to go. He had to attend a convention in Texas. We all had fun those two days. It was almost magical. None of us talked about any men. None of us spoke of Mike, Rex, or Tom. That was strange. Having girl time. Michelle had a great time. She dressed up like Snow White and at her birthday party, the seven dwarfs acted out a scene with her from the classic tale. I couldn't help but cry. My little girl was so happy. Now Michelle could go back to school and tell her classmates how she not only went to Disney World, but she celebrated her birthday there. Orlando was so beautiful, with all the palm trees and the characters designed from flowers on the landscape. Michelle was the happiest six-year-old in the first grade. She was so excited. My role had gone from being a mother to also being a father and a friend.

A month later, Michelle and I attended the weddings in Loxley. Janie and Timmy had a double wedding, the most incredible thing I had ever seen. It was like a scene right out of a romantic movie. Edna and I shipped the wedding gowns to Janie and Darla from the shop. They were so beautiful. Long white gowns with lace. The bridesmaids wore lavender dresses. All of the men wore white tuxedos. Rex looked so handsome and mature. Janie asked me to be her matron of honor, but I decided not to. My stomach was so big and just my luck, I would have gone into labor during the ceremony. I sat in the audience and took several photos. Mama was so beautiful. She was the matron of honor for Janie. She wore a strapless purple dress. Her hair was pinned up with little white daisies and baby's breath. Tom Farraday, oh my goodness; he was so handsome standing there in his white tuxedo, like Prince Charming. I could see where Mike got his good looks.

Tom walked Janie down the aisle, and gave her away to Rex. A complete fairy tale. Last but not least, my little angel, Michelle, was absolutely gorgeous. She wore a purple dress and her hair was filled with Shirley Temple curls. She threw little daisies as she walked down the aisle. The wedding was held outside in front of the barn on a beautiful autumn day. The sun was bright and shining with a magical glow. There was a little breeze in the air that afternoon, and by nightfall everyone needed a jacket or a sweater. Winter was definitely moving in to Loxley. The reception was held at Mama and Janie's house. They even had some dancing going on in the barn. Everyone was so happy. Edna and Joe had a great time.

I noticed that Tom Farraday was still living in the house with Mama. There was a rumor floating around that he gave Timmy and Darla his house as a wedding present. Now that sounded pretty interesting. I hoped Mama didn't end up pregnant. Ha ha ha…That would be funny. Regardless of all the beauty I witnessed that day, a part of me still felt like marrying

Mike at such an early age was the worst mistake of my life. I just couldn't stop crying. My heart ached for the love and peace that surrounded me that day.

Two weeks later, the family in Loxley drove down to Florida to see me give birth to an eight-pound, five-ounce baby boy. Michael Jr. Unlike Michelle, Michael Jr. was born with a bald head. No hair anywhere. He had the biggest blue eyes. The innocence of life is seen through the eyes of a child. I knew when I looked at Michael Jr., he would never be like his father. Respectable, loving, kind, selfless, these are the things I see when I look into the eyes of my baby. Mike finally came by the hospital after I left him several messages that my water had broken and I was going into labor. He wasn't there to see the birth of either of our children.

Strangely, I noticed when Mike opened my hospital room door, the young man with the blonde hair was standing outside. For some reason, this guy seemed evil. Those hazel eyes and that half-crooked smile that he wore gave me the feeling that he was up to no good. Mike held our son. The minute he picked him up, the baby started to cry. Mike smiled at him, tried talking to him, but the baby wouldn't stop crying.

"Here, Sara, make him stop crying. Feed him or something, just make him shut up."

Janie and Mama were in the room visiting me and the baby at the time. Mike handed me the baby. He never acknowledged the fact that my family was even there. No hellos, good evenings, nothing. Janie took the baby and walked around the room singing to him. He immediately stopped crying. Janie agreed that Michael Jr. looked just like my brother Timmy when he was a baby. I could sense that Mike was uncomfortable being in the room with my family.

"Sara, I'm heading out. I've got to go by the club and do some inventory." Mike kissed me on the forehead. "I'll see you later."

"Goodbye, Mike. Thanks for fitting us into your busy schedule."

Mike was in such a big hurry to leave, he didn't pay any attention to the comment that I made. Just as he opened the door, Tom walked into the room.

"Well, son, I haven't seen you in a long time. We've got a lot to talk about."

Mike stood there for a minute as if he was thinking of something unique to say. All of a sudden, out of the blue, he grabbed Tom and started to hug him. He even started to cry. Oh my goodness, was the great Michael Farraday crying? I got out of bed and walked over to Janie. Pretending to be playing with the baby, I glanced over at Mike. Not one tear in his eyes. Mike was putting on one of his better performances. Yes, he could be a real live drama king when he wanted to be. Today was the day that we all got our money's worth with that performance.

He let go of his dad and just walked out of the room. Poor Tom...Mike had him convinced that he was just so upset that he couldn't say a word. But I knew better. He was trying to exit stage left as soon as possible. All I could do was stand there and shake my head in disbelief.

CHAPTER EIGHTEEN:

Trying to Survive

Two months had gone by. Michael Jr. was growing fast. He was such a good baby. He rarely cried at all unless Mike tried to hold him. It's as though he could sense the evil inside of Mike. The time had come for me to get back out into the work force again. I had no idea what to do about daycare. Everything was so expensive. Although I made a pretty good salary at my job, it was still hard trying to budget all the bills and take care of a new baby. Mike was still being Mike. He didn't contribute to paying bills, buying groceries, or helping with any of the children's expenses. I had pretty much run out of options. I loved him with all my heart, but it just wasn't enough. I told him I would be by his side through thick and thin, but he was never there for me and the children. When I tried to talk to him, he always started an argument and then tried to beat me.

The Peck sisters next door offered to keep Michael Jr. for free in order for me to return to work. They were nice ladies. I mistook their concern for nosiness. They just wanted to help and I really did appreciate that. Michelle liked spending time with the neighbors. She enjoyed talking to them and playing at their house. They had several antique dolls and a huge dollhouse. On Saturday mornings, the sisters would bake cookies and pretend to have a tea party with Michelle as the guest of honor. I never told Mike that Michelle was going over to visit the sisters. He would be angry. He hated the neighbors and felt like we shouldn't have any dealings with any of them.

One evening Ms. Abigail came by the house to bring some spaghetti. I heard a small knock at the front door. As I opened the door, I saw Ms. Abigail standing there with a huge pot in her hands.

"Hello, Ms. Abigail. Oh my goodness. That wouldn't happen to be a pot of spaghetti, now would it?"

"Yes it is. I also brought some garlic toast to go along with it."

"Ms. Abigail, you are an angel. I haven't had any good spaghetti since my mama cooked some for the family a few months ago."

We both walked into the kitchen and placed everything on the stove. Boy was I happy to see her. There are only two people on this earth that make good spaghetti, my mama and Ms. Abigail.

"Now, Sara, I'm going to head back to the house. Don't forget, as soon you're ready to go back to work, my sister and I are looking forward to taking care of Michael Jr. He is such a wonderful little baby. We love him so much."

"Thank you so much for the offer, Ms. Abigail. Are you sure that he's not gonna be too much for the two of you to handle?"

"No. We look forward to helping you. We love Michael Jr. There is something special about him. His soul is pure and his heart is good. He will bring love and peace to those that surround him. You have really been blessed, Sara Farraday."

"Can I offer you any type of payment?"

"No ma'am. Just bring him a few diapers and his formula, and we will supply the rest. I know that people have called my sister and I different names all of our lives. Witches, hanks, we have even been called lesbians. My sister got married when she was young, just like you. Walter Baxter was her husband. He was a nice man. They had their entire future mapped out. Two years went by. They decided to try and start a family. Walter became sick one night. He thought it was heartburn from something that he had eaten earlier that day.

"My sister tried to get him to go to the hospital, but he said that the pain would pass on," she continued. "He took some medicine and sat in his recliner chair to watch the late-night news. Against her better judgment, my sister went to bed, thinking that Walter would be there soon, just like he had did every night. My sister slept hard that night. She woke up about four in the morning and noticed that Walter had never come to bed. She got up and walked into the living room.

"There he was. Walter Baxter died that night while sitting in his recliner chair. My sister never forgave herself for not insisting that Walter go to the hospital. The autopsy never revealed why Walter died. It took Amanda several years to get over losing that man. After she finally got herself together, she decided she would never marry again, and she didn't."

She went on with her story, her thoughts firmly in the past.

"I, on the other hand, loved boys when I was a young girl," she said. "I would wear the sexiest dresses that I could find. All of the girls in my class called me a slut. I didn't care. They were just jealous because I was pretty. Flirting, that's all I did. Sex was the last thing on my mind. Getting a proper education was my first concern. I always had a fascination with dolls. A Clothing designer or a dollhouse maker, that's what I chose to do for my career.

"My dreams were put on hold for five years of my life. I went out to the ice cream shop with one of my male college professors. We were going to have a few scoops of ice cream and talk about some of my clothing designs. It seemed harmless. My mother was strict and didn't like for me to be out after eleven. It was about ten o'clock when I suggested to the professor that it was time for him to take me home. He asked me why was I in such a hurry to get home so early on a Friday night. I told him that he didn't have to face my mother. Daddy didn't mind, but Mother was determined to raise the proper ladies in her house. He said he understood and paid for the ice cream.

"While he was driving me home, he told me he wanted to stop by his office for a minute and get some magazines that he had picked up in Paris. He said I was his favorite student and I had a big chance of going far in the fashion world. His office was located just down the street from the college campus. The professor parked in the driveway and got out of the car. He started walking toward the office door with his keys, but he turned around. He came back to the car and said that it would take less time if I came in and helped him look for the magazines. Not thinking, all I wanted to do was get home on time, so I agreed to go into his office and help him look for the magazines. I was so honored that he thought of me as his favorite student. I just knew that my career dreams would come true.

"When I walked into what I was told was an office, I saw living room furniture and a kitchen off to the side," she continued. "It looked like a small house instead of an office. He told me that since he was single, the college offered him the office, but it was big enough for him to use as a house. He told me to come into the back room, that's where his office was located. When I went into the room, the professor grabbed me from behind and pushed me onto a bed. He quickly got on top of me and told me if I did what he wanted, then I wouldn't get hurt. I had never been that scared before in my life. I was only nineteen years old. He started to reach his hands under my dress. He raped me that night. I couldn't say a word."

She paused for a minute, visibly upset.

"How could this have happened to me?" she asked. "All I wanted was to get a magazine. He put me in his car and drove me home. He told me not to tell anyone or I would regret it and then drove off like a bat out of hell. My mother was standing at the door when I walked up the front steps. She immediately started screaming for help. My clothes had been ripped and blood was all over my dress and legs. She knew what had happened. Despite the professor's threats, he didn't know my mother. She held me in her arms in the backseat of the car as my father drove me to the hospital. Everyone was crying.

"When I got to the emergency room, the doctor said that I had some internal bleeding. I had to have an emergency hysterectomy for them to stop the bleeding. The professor was arrested and sent to prison, but it didn't change the fact that my life had been destroyed. It took five years of counseling before I started to feel human again. That was about the same time that my sister's husband died. My father bought us a house together and since then, it has always just been the two of us. We both got jobs working in a fabric shop. A friend of my father hired me to make clothes for one of his shops. I worked there for a few years, but I still had a passion for dolls.

"My sister and I had collected so many dolls during the years, we started a doll-making shop. We loved it, and the people; I didn't realize that so many adults collected dolls. We kept the shop open for thirty years, before we decided to retire and just enjoy each other's company."

"Ms. Abigail, I didn't realize that you and your sister had gone through so much. I am so sorry."

"You don't have to be sorry, child. We are fine and we enjoy life every day. Don't feel sorry for us; just let us be a part of your life."

Mike came through the front door. I was so involved in Ms. Abigail's story, I didn't hear his car in the driveway. Ms. Abigail glanced over at Mike. "Hello, Michael."

Mike didn't say a word. He walked into the bedroom and slammed the door as if she was not standing there. "Well, I've better get to the house."

"Let me walk you to the door."

I couldn't help but hug her again once we walked out onto the front porch. "Thank you again for the food and the conversation."

"You are more than welcome. Please let me know when you're ready to go to work. My sister and I are looking so forward to taking care of Michael Jr. You be careful, Sara. Talk with you later."

"Goodbye, Ms. Abigail."

I watched her walk next door to her house. How they must have felt growing up. I knew that they had a story, but I didn't know how sad it was. As I walked back into the house, Mike was standing behind the door.

"Mike, you're home a little early, aren't you?"

He walked up to me and said, "I know that you're not gonna let those old bitches take care of my son."

"Mike, they are nice women. You've just never taken the time to get to know them. Michelle likes them a lot."

"You mean Michelle has been going over to their house?"

"Yes, some days they let her come over to play with their doll collection."

"Why didn't you tell me about this?" I noticed the tone in his voice was getting a little louder.

I held his hand and replied, "They are sweet and they're good with children, plus they offered to keep Michael Jr. for free. Sweetie, it's taking all of the money that I make just to keep this family going."

Mike pulled his hand away from mine. "I'm tired of you doing things behind my back. I don't like those old hags. They stare at me. Piercing a hole through my heart as if they were looking at my soul."

Mike just kept rambling on. He was beginning to talk foolish and I found myself getting tired of this conversation.

"You mean to tell me they've been taking care of my kids? Hell, no! I'll take care of Michael Jr. myself."

Before I knew it, words just kept racing out of my mouth. "Are you crazy? How in the hell are you gonna take care of a baby? You can't even buy milk or diapers for him. You don't give me any money for the bills or for food. The last time you bought Michelle an outfit was over two years ago. Mike, you're never at home. A strange woman came in here and kicked your butt. She took your money out of your wallet. You're not responsible enough to take care of our son. I don't need you to babysit; I need you to be a man and step up to the plate. You have a family that you should be taking care of financially."

"You bitch! Who do you think you're talking to?" I could see the rage building up inside of him. His eyes were black as the night. His breathing was hard and fierce. I could hear his heart pounding inside his chest. Blood was trickling down from his hands; his fist was so tight that his fingernails had begun to cut into the palms of his hands. Not knowing what was in store for me, I had to release and speak what had been trapped inside my heart for the last six years.

"Mike, everything was just fine when we got married, but when you got that job at the nightclub, everything changed, including you. We don't exist anymore."

He slowly started to walk toward me. "Mike, I just want you to help me a little more." As I gently kept backing away, looking him straight in his eyes, I said, "Mike, I love you. I just want us to be happy."

Yes, I was probably about to get the worst beating I had ever received from my husband, but I had to tell him what was in my heart and on my mind. Mike jumped toward me, attempting to put his hands around my neck. Not thinking about what I was doing, my first response was to grab his hands.

"Let go of my hands, Sara."

Staring him in the eyes, I held on to his hands for dear life. I knew if I were to let go, there is no telling what he might have done to me. We struggled around the living room. We finally ended up in the bedroom. "Damn it, Sara, let go of me."

I was so scared. For goodness' sake, please give me strength to hold on, I prayed. All of a sudden, the doorbell rang. Yes... yes, a miracle. *Ding dong*. Someone was at the door.

"Hey, Sara. Mike, are you there? Let me in. This is Tom. Open the door."

Oh my goodness. It was Tom Farraday. We continued to two-step around the bedroom a few more seconds. I then let go of Mike's hands and ran like lightning toward the living room. Quickly I opened the front door.

"Hello, Mr. Tom." I was completely out of breath as if I had just run a marathon race. Looking down at the floor, continuing to breathe hysterically, I said, "Come in, Mr. Tom."

"Sara, what's going on? Honey, take your time and catch your breath."

By that time, Mike was walking out of the bedroom. I glanced up at Tom with tears in my eyes. He reached into his pocket and pulled out a roll of money. He opened my hand and placed it inside.

"Sara, take the kids to the park and out for dinner." He had a look of determination on his face. His eyes were on Mike. They stared at each other as if they were preparing for the biggest duel of their lives. I stood there for a few seconds wondering who would be the last man standing. I wasn't sure if I should leave the two of them there together or not.

"Sara, take the kids and do what I say. Old Mike and I need some alone time."

"Yes, sir, Mr. Tom," I replied. Quickly I ran into Michelle's bedroom.

"Michelle, grab your sweater and backpack, we're going out for dinner." Michael Jr. was asleep in his bed. I picked him up and grabbed his diaper bag.

"Come on, Michelle. Grandpa will visit with you and your brother later. He needs to talk to Daddy right now. We'll bring him some ice cream back."

"Alright, Mommy. Bye, Daddy. Bye, Grandpa."

Neither Mike nor Tom said a word. The tension was so thick in that room at that moment, no knife in the world could have begun to cut it. The kids and I went outside. Tom shut the door behind us. As I walked to the car, I became more and more hesitant about leaving those two alone at the house together. Although Mike did need someone to set him on the right track, I just wasn't sure if Tom could do it after all of these years.

Ms. Abigail was standing on her front porch watering her flowers. An idea popped into my head at that moment. "Ms. Abigail."

"Hello, Sara. Oh...Look at those two angels."

"Ms. Abigail, can you watch the two of them for a little while? Something just came up that I need to take care of."

"Go ahead, Sara, do what you need to do. I'll watch the little ones."

"Mommy, I thought we were going out to dinner?"

"Did someone mention dinner? My sister and I were just about to prepare some big juicy cheeseburgers with all the trimmings. How does that sound, Michelle?"

"I love cheeseburgers."

"Good. You can come in and help us prepare them."

"Thank you so much, Ms. Abigail."

"Is everything alright, really?"

"Pray for me and my family."

Ms. Abigail took the kids into the house.

CHAPTER NINETEEN:

Tom's Confession

I got into my car, drove down the street, and parked between two oak trees at the corner. Sara Farraday, what are you doing, I asked myself. I made my way back to the house and quietly eased onto the front porch. They were talking pretty loud, so I didn't have a problem hearing what was being said. The curtain was slightly open in the living room window. As I glanced in, I noticed that Mike was still standing near the bedroom door.

"Old man, you just wasted your time coming here. I'm not in the mood for your crap today."

"Son, I just wanted to come here and tell you that I'm sorry. I'm sorry for everything that I put you through. Mike, I should have been there for you all these years instead of just giving you everything that you wanted and letting you run wild. Your mama loved you with all of her heart and soul. She made me promise to take care of you before she died. I just can't forgive myself if I don't honor her wishes."

"What about my wishes, Tom Farraday? Why didn't the both of you just let me die? You think you gave me everything I wanted? Is that what you just said? Let's see, what did you give me? Alright, I remember now. You gave me money and a car, so I could never be at home. Then you gave me Grandpa's house, so I could leave your home. Yeah, I remember now. Thanks, good old Dad."

"Your mother gave her life in order for you to have life."

"Well, I didn't ask her to bring me into this sick world. I didn't ask her to do a damn thing."

"You watch your mouth, boy."

As I glanced into the window, I saw Tom walking toward Mike. The two of them were pretty much standing in each other's face.

"All your mama ever wanted was for her son to grow up and be a good man."

"And what are you trying to say? I'm not a good man? Michael Farraday is not a good man? Well, guess what, Daddy, neither are you. My grandfather was more of a man than you will ever be. Tell me, did you ever wonder why my mama named me after your father instead of after you? Oh…

Don't look so damn surprised. I heard Aunt Edna and Uncle Joe talking about it when I was a little kid."

"I don't know what you're talking about."

"You don't remember when you and your new wife had to stay with your daddy? All of those business trips that you had to make and those late-night meetings you had to attend in order to build your empire? Tom Farraday, who do you think was keeping your sweet young bride company all of those nights? Guess what, it wasn't Mr. Sandman!"

Mike started laughing hysterically. Tom gently sat down on the sofa.

"I know the truth," Mike said. "I've always known that your father was my father too. So I guess that makes me your brother instead of your son.

"You know, Tom, I guess you are a good man. I probably would have killed the bitch, except for her having cancer and all. Did you plan for her to die while giving birth to me, or were you just hoping she would die? It worked out pretty good. You had no one to explain anything to. Everyone thought I was your son. The only person who knew that you were sterile was your sister Edna. I guess you just couldn't stand the fact that your own wife got pregnant by your daddy. Is that why you hated me? Why didn't you just confront them both and tell them you knew they were sleeping around? I know, she got you with that dying wish crap, didn't she? You started to feel sorry for her. See, that's where you messed up. Women ain't good for much. They will screw up your life! Then time you start to smack 'em around a little, they want to call the cops."

"Mike! Stop it!"

"Stop what?" Mike replied. "You don't want to play tell the truth anymore Daddy? Doggone it! I've said that word so much. Daddy. It's gonna be hard for me to think of you as just plain old Tom."

"I did it for you, Michael."

"Say what?"

"When I married your mother, yes, I had a lot of hopes and dreams. She was the most beautiful woman that I had ever laid eyes on. I wanted to treat her like a queen. The ranch house was still being built in Loxley, so we ended up staying here with Daddy, in this house for a few months. Elizabeth and Edna were good friends. The two of them came up with the idea to open a dress shop. She was so happy. I knew I was leaving her alone a lot, but I wanted to give her the world. My father always swore that I would never amount to anything. I had to prove him wrong and I did.

In my heart, I feel as if he purposely took advantage of Elizabeth's shyness and seduced her. My father wasn't a good man. He treated my mother like dirt until the day she left him.

"When I was fourteen years old, my father and I went horseback riding. It was my first time. I hated it and Daddy knew I hated it. So every weekend he'd take me horseback riding. He'd show me different horses and introduce me to some of the richest men that owned these horses. One day, I started to like it. I even started suggesting that Daddy and I go horseback riding.

"There was this one horse that wouldn't let anyone come near him," he went on. "The most beautiful creature that I had ever seen. He was as black as the night. Wild in every way, but still a sight to behold. Daddy told me to ride it one evening. I told Daddy that the horse was too wild and would never let anyone ride it. He insisted I ride that damn horse. He even went as far as to try to help me get on the saddle. I begged Daddy to stop. Hell, everyone standing around begged him to stop. But he was determined that I ride that horse, right then and there. When I finally got on the horse, the horse threw me onto the ground. I tried to get up, but I was in too much pain.

"When I got to the hospital, the doctors told me I would be alright, but I would never be able to father a child due to testicular internal damage. After all those years, I didn't think about it anymore until I met Elizabeth. I just figured that if I could give her everything she wanted financially, then maybe we could just adopt a child. It's my fault; I should have told her that I was sterile before we got married. When the ranch was finished and your mother and I moved in, I planned on telling her the truth that night. That's when she told me that she was pregnant. I immediately knew who the father was. It was a hard pill to swallow, but I just pretended that I didn't know the truth. About a month later, Elizabeth was diagnosed with breast cancer. She was a good woman, Mike. I can't blame her for any of this."

"You are stupid," Mike said. "How can you sit there and say that you can't blame her for any of this? Let me see, she was screwing around with your daddy, she got pregnant by your daddy and forgot to tell you, and then she died and left you holding the bag, or I should say the baby. But you don't blame her for any of this, right?"

"She was the first woman I ever loved and I will always hold a special place for her in my heart."

"Bravo, bravo," Mike replied as he clapped his hands. "What a speech. I'm glad you're not my daddy. You're such a freaking loser, Tom."

Oh my goodness. I couldn't believe I was standing there outside the window listening to this conversation.

"I promised Elizabeth that I would watch out for you, Mike, and I'm gonna keep my word."

"You can save it. I'm not your problem and I can take care of myself. Now, I think it's time that you left my house, Tommy boy. I've got things to do."

"I don't care if I'm your father or not, you're gonna listen to me. You better not put your hands on Sara again."

"It's her fault. She won't do anything that I tell her. I have to show her that I'm the man and she will answer to me. No woman is gonna tell me what to do or when to do it. Bitches think that they can shed a few tears and just control the world, but I'm not gonna let them control me."

"Mike. Listen to yourself. Son, you need help. Let me try and get you some counseling or at least try going to an AA meeting. I'll go with you."

"Are you trying to call me crazy? You think I'm crazy. Oh, I'll show you crazy."

Mike had completely lost it. He grabbed Tom up from the sofa by his shirt collar. In fear of what would happen next, I dialed 911 on my cell phone.

"Get your hands off of me, Mike. I'm warning you."

"Or what, Tom Farraday, you're gonna kill your little brother? Is that what you want to say?"

Tom pushed Mike off of him. By that time, I heard sirens. A police car quickly turned into the driveway. I ran toward the neighbor's house and hid out of sight. *Knock, knock.* "Who is it?"

"It's the Henderson Police. Sir, we got a complaint that there might be some type of disturbance going on here."

Tom walked over and opened the front door. "Hi, officer. My name is Tom Farraday. My son and I were having a deep discussion. I guess we got a little too loud. I was just on my way home."

"Mike Farraday. Is that you?"

"Yes, it's me."

"Didn't I just pull you over the other night for speeding?"

"Yeah, you did, officer, but everything is alright. Just like my daddy said, we were having a discussion, and we just got a little too loud, that's all."

"Sir, do you mind if we come in and just look around?"

"As a matter of fact, I do mind."

"Where's your wife, Mike?" the officer asked.

"She took the kids out to dinner. She's not here."

"Officers, there's no one here but my son and me and I'm heading home," Tom said. "I've got about a two-hour drive to Loxley. I do apologize for any inconvenience."

"Since everything seems to be alright at this time, then we'll be leaving." The officer looked at Tom and asked, "Sir, do you mind leaving the premises first?"

"No, I don't mind. Mike, I'm sorry. I hope that we can sit down and clear the air about everything. If you need anything, please call me. I love you, son."

Mike just stood there on the front porch smiling. Tom got into his truck and drove away. The police stood there talking to Mike for a while and then they left. So stunned by everything that I had overheard, I didn't know what to do. I went down the street to my car and slowly drove it into the driveway. I desperately wanted to talk to Mike, hoping that he could somehow bring himself to trust me enough to confide in me. My throat was choked up. What would I say? I opened the front door slowly to find Mike sitting on the sofa.

"Baby, are you alright? Did your dad leave?"

"Yes, that idiot is gone."

In my attempts to comfort Mike, I went over and knelt down in front of him. I attempted to hold his hands. Mike stood up from the sofa and pulled me up from the floor. He slapped me as hard as he could, over and over again. As I went down to the floor, I couldn't help but wonder where this was coming from.

"Mike, please don't hit me, please." By that time, my mouth was filled with the taste of blood.

"I'm not gonna hit you, Sara, I'm just gonna kick your ass."
He kicked me in the stomach, the back. He just wouldn't stop. It all happened so fast. The very thought of screaming didn't enter my mind.

CHAPTER TWENTY:

Mike Goes to Jail

It had to have been at least an hour later. I found myself awakened by the sweet little voice of Ms. Abigail. "Sara. Sara. Wake up, child."

I opened my eyes. I was still lying on the floor. Ms. Abigail was cleaning the blood from my face. "Sara, are you able to move?"

"Let me just lie here for a little while longer." I hurt so badly. Probably a few broken ribs, but I thought I would survive. "Is Mike still here?"

"No...That animal drove off about an hour ago. I saw you coming back to the house from my window. I got worried about you, so when I saw Mike leave, that's when I came over and found you lying on the floor in blood. Sara, you have to call the police. Honey, you need to go to the hospital."

"If I call the police, they'll take my children away from me."

"No, they won't. I bet Mike told you that, didn't he? We won't let anyone take your children away from you."

"Where are you going, Ms. Abigail?"

"I'm calling the police."

"But Mike may come after you."

"Sara, did it ever occur to you that not everyone is afraid of Mike Farraday?"

Before I knew it, the police and an ambulance had arrived at the house. I went to the hospital and the police went to look for Mike. The doctors said that I had a couple of broken ribs and would be pretty sore for a few days. Broken ribs and I were definitely not strangers. The sisters kept the kids while I was at the hospital. I didn't want to tell the police what had happened, but the evidence was on my face and body.

A strange thing happened. Mama and Janie showed up at the hospital.

"Mama, how did you know I was here?"

"Mike called Tom and told him that he had beaten you up pretty bad and said that he was turning himself in to the police. Tom went to the police station, and your sister and I came here to see you. Sara, are you alright? Why didn't you tell us that Mike was hitting on you again?"

"Mama, I don't think he ever stopped," Janie replied as she stood there looking as if she didn't want to be there. "You're not going back to that house. Do you hear me? The doctor said you could leave in the morning. We're gonna get those kids and head to Loxley. Mike is crazy. Tom told me a lot of interesting things about Michael Farraday and you're not going back to him."

"Did he tell you that Mike is not his son? Did he tell you how he lied to everyone all those years, Mama?"

"Sara Ramsey, I don't believe you. This man has darn near killed you and you still want to lie there and blame other people for his sick behavior. What happened to you? Is it my fault that you somehow feel that you have to hold onto this man? If I did anything, anything in my life to cause you to feel this way, then I am sorry! I am so sorry."

"Mama, don't beg her," Janie replied. "She's with that drunk because she wants to be with him."

All I could do was lay there and cry. It was true. The only reason I put up with Mike was because I kept holding onto the thought that maybe one day he would be the man of my dreams. I turned my face toward the wall, ashamed to talk to my own family. Afraid of what they would think of a woman whose husband hit her for no apparent reason. It was my fault. I should never have gone into the house after the police left. He had already been provoked by Tom. I should have left well enough alone. Why did I do these things?

"Sara, we're gonna leave and let you get some rest. We have a hotel room across the street from the hospital. Your sister and I will be back in the morning to pick you up. Sweetheart, please just get some rest. I love you, Sara."

"Thank you, Mama. Thanks for coming here to see me. I love you too."

"Goodnight, baby," Mama replied as she gently kissed my forehead. Janie walked out of the room in disgust. Lying there thinking, I couldn't figure out for the life of me why Mike would turn himself in to the police. Tom would probably pay his bail. There was something strange going on. The drama king had some plan in mind, and knowing me, I would probably fall for it, hook, line, and sinker.

The nurses were in and out of my room all night long. They took my vital signs, blood, and asked me a ton of questions. I think most of them were just curious to see the woman who had been beaten by her husband. Hearing them whispering among themselves when they thought I was asleep. Tossing and turning half the night in this uncomfortable bed. Sleep was definitely not in the plan for me.

Morning came around pretty fast. Just as I finished my breakfast, Mama and Tom knocked on my door.

"Good morning, sweetheart," Mama said. "How do you feel this morning?"

"Hi, Mama. Hello, Tom. I guess I'm alright."

"I went by your neighbor's house and told them that we would be by later today to pick up the kids. They are such nice ladies. I'm just glad that they were there for you and the kids."

"Tom, what's going on with Mike? Did he really turn himself in to the police?"

"Yes, he did, Sara, but by the time I arrived at the police station, his friend Chris had paid the bail."

"Who is Chris?"

"Tall blonde-headed guy with green eyes."

That guy sounded familiar, but his eyes were hazel, just like a cat.

"I followed them to the house," Tom said. "Mike promised the police that he would move out of the house and start attending AA meetings. That's one of the reasons that they let him out on bail. He said he'd be staying with Chris."

"He moved out?"

"Well...He did take a couple of suitcases. Sara, look, I know somehow you overheard that conversation between Mike and myself. You know that I'm not his father. He reminds me so much of our father, Michael Farraday Sr. There is a sickness inside of Mike. An anger that lies deep inside of his heart. Sara, I agree with your mama. I think you should just take the kids and come with us back to Loxley. If Mike is sincere about being your husband, then he will get the help that he needs in order to hold onto you and those two beautiful children. But I don't think you should stay here in Florida. Let him come to you when he's ready to finally be your husband."

"But what about my house? I can't just leave my house. What about Michelle's school? My job at the shop, you want me to walk away and never look back?"

"Honey, you can find another house and job in Loxley, and you know that Michelle can be transferred to another school."

"No, I can't leave here, Mama. Since Mike is living with his friend, there is no reason that the kids and I can't go back to our home."

"Sara, what is wrong with you? I raised you to be a smart, responsible woman. Never in a million years would I have imagined that you would allow some childhood fantasy to destroy your life."

We heard a loud knock at the door. "Come in," I said.

"Hello, I'm Dr. Howard. Mrs. Farraday?"

"Yes, I'm Sara Farraday."

"I looked at your chart and it seems that you've got a couple of broken ribs, which will heal in about two to three weeks. There's going to be some soreness and pain. I'm going to write you a prescription for some antibiotics and something for pain. Take the Levaquin, one tablet twice a day for seven days, and the Lortab, one tablet every four to six hours as needed for pain. You can follow up with your primary care physician in about two weeks. Other than that, you are free to leave. The nurse will be in and explain the discharge instructions to you and give you your prescriptions. Well, Mrs. Farraday, you take better care of yourself and let's try not to meet again under these circumstances. Good-bye."

"Goodbye, Doctor, and thank you for everything."

"Well, Sara, what's it gonna be? Are you gonna get dressed and let us take you to Loxley or what?"

"No! Mama, please, I just want to go home."

As much as I love my mama, I had become tired and fed up with her thoughts of taking me and my kids back to Loxley.

"Julia, why don't we step outside and let the nurse help Sara get dressed, and then we will take her to her house," Tom said.

Mama and Tom stepped out into the hallway. "But, Tom, she can't go back there."

"Julia, Mike is gone. He's staying with his friend. She'll be alright. Plus, she's right; she can't just take Michelle out of school in the middle of the semester. Julia, I'm gonna be honest with you, if you make her go back to Loxley, she will hate you forever, just like Mike hates me."

"But, Tom, this situation is different from what's going on between you and Mike."

"Trust me, Julia, she'll hate you if you try to make her leave Mike. She has to do it on her own."

"That's what I'm afraid of; she may never do it on her own. Tom, I'm so scared that he is gonna hurt her or even kill her one day."

"Now you listen to me: I promise you, even if I have to ride to Henderson every day to check on Sara, nothing is going to happen to her. I give you my word, Julia Ramsey. Let Sara go back to her house. Besides, if Mike goes anywhere near that house, he will be arrested on the spot."

"Thank you so much, Tom. I'm so glad you are a part of my life. I love you." She kissed him gently on the lips.

"Julia, I love you and there is nothing I wouldn't do for you or your family." The two hugged and came back into my room.

"Sara, are you ready?" Mama asked.

"It depends on where we're going."

"Tom and I are going to take you to your house. Against my better judgment, I wouldn't want you to take Michelle out of school in the middle of the year. But if you need anything, you better call me, young lady."

"Yes, ma'am."

Mama and I hugged. I was so glad she stopped pushing the issue about me going back to Loxley.

"Mrs. Farraday, these are your discharge instructions and your two prescriptions. If you have any unusual pain, coughing, or spitting up blood, please come back to the emergency room immediately."

"Thank you, nurse."

"Transportation is here with your wheelchair. They will take you out front to the discharge ramp. Are you all parked out front?"

"Yes, we are," Tom replied.

"Alright then, the two of you can wait for Mrs. Farraday out front."

"Nurse, I don't need a wheelchair."

"It's hospital policy."

"Go ahead, Sara. Tom and I will meet you at the car."

As I was wheeled down the hospital hall, I noticed how dull and gray the walls were. I'd been to this hospital before, but it never dawned on me how bleak and depressing this place looked.

Once we got to the exit doors, Tom helped me into the back seat of Mama's car. The drive was long and quiet, giving me the time I needed to try to understand what was happening to me. We arrived at the house. I wanted desperately to go to the neighbors and see the kids, but I couldn't let them see me looking like this. Plus, I had no answers. Michelle, being as curious as she was, would probably ask me a million questions. I had to find answers to my own questions right now. As I walked into the house, everything seemed so different. Walking into the bedroom, I noticed that Mike's clothes and his personal items were all gone.

"Honey, you've got food in the refrigerator, but Tom and I can go to the store for you if you need anything."

"No, Mama, I just want to lie down and get some rest. Thank you for getting my prescriptions filled for me."

"Sara, your mother and I are gonna go next door and check on the kids," Tom said. "We'll take them some more clothes for the rest of the week. Those Peck sisters are wonderful. They said they would come by and check on you as well."

"Don't worry about going to work, honey, Tom talked to Edna and she said for you to take as much time as you need."

"Mama, where is Janie?"

"She drove back to Loxley last night."

"She hates me, doesn't she?"

"No, sweetheart. Janie's been having a little bit of a stomach virus lately. You know, I wouldn't be surprised if she was pregnant." Mama smiled at me. "Well, we're gonna get out of here so you can rest. Call us if you need anything. I love you, honey."

Mama and Tom walked out the front door. All I could do was stand in the bedroom with a blank stare on my face. I didn't even tell Mama and Tom good-bye. All I could think about was the fact that Mike was gone. I know I should feel happy, but why did I feel so sad and lonely?

Oh man, my side hurt like the devil. You guys are my friends now, I said to the bottle of pain pills I was holding in my hand. I decided to take two of those babies and go to bed. As I closed my eyes, I prayed that this nightmare would be over in the morning.

CHAPTER TWENTY-ONE:

Living With Myself

A week had gone by as I desperately tried to deal with the silence in the house. I felt so depressed. The sisters brought the kids over to visit with me. My face looked a lot better. Seeing their little smiles made me feel much better. They were the only sunshine I had in my cloudy life. The soreness and pain was slowly fading away.

I couldn't help but think about Mike. How can someone you love cause you so much heartache and pain? Get out of this bed, Sara, and stop feeling sorry for yourself, I ordered myself. I had two children to raise, with or without Mike. A hot shower sounded like heaven right about then, since I had lain in that bed for a week. It was time to get my butt up and get back to the real world.

After my shower, I noticed that the house was screaming out for a good cleaning. My body felt better; maybe I could do a little dusting and put the dishes in the dishwasher. Before I could get started doing anything, I heard a loud knock at the front door. Who could that be this time of morning? It was probably Tom. I had noticed his truck sitting outside the house every day this week.

"I'm coming."

As I opened the door, oh my goodness, it was Chris. The tall man with the blond hair and hazel eyes was standing at my front door.

"Sara, my name is Chris. I'm a friend of Mike's. He told me to give this to you. Please don't tell anyone that I was here."

Chris handed me a letter and walked back to a cab he had waiting for him in the street. So that was Mike's new friend. He had a deep voice. His face still looked so familiar, as if I had seen him before in the past. Could I have seen him somewhere when I was living in Loxley? One day, I would figure out where I first saw this mystery man by the name of Chris. Desperately wanting to read the letter, I rushed back into the house and sat on the sofa. There were four pages stuffed in a small white envelope.

Dear Sara,

First I want to apologize for everything that I have done. I am so sorry for hurting you. I was just so angry with Tom; I had no right to take it out on you. I thought it would be best if I moved out of the house for a while. I started attending AA meetings on Monday nights. I have also been talking to a counselor. He has helped me to face a lot of the problems that I couldn't deal with on my own.

A lot of the drinking and the violence was from the fact that I miss my mother. I never got a chance to see her or even get to hear her voice. My dad hated me for all these years because he blamed me for her death. Sara, I had no one. No one to talk to. No one to hug me. No one to tuck me in at night. I never had a father/son talk. I envied you. You grew up on a farm with people that loved you. I think a part of me was jealous. For once in my life, I have someone to love and I don't know how to handle it. The problem is not you, Sara. It never was. The problem is me. I need to learn how to love, so that I can be a husband for you and a father for my children. I don't know how long it's gonna take and if you want to divorce me, then I'll understand.

The court hearing is in two weeks. I know that you have to testify. When I turned myself in, I told the police that I hit you and you fell on the floor, causing your cuts and bruises. I know that I lied to them, but I really need some help, Sara. If I'm locked up in prison, I can't get the help that I need. The prison system doesn't help those guys. They come out of prison doing the same things that they got locked up for. I want to change and be a better man. The only way I can do that is if you testify that I only hit you once since we've been married. I hate to put you in this position, and if you want to tell the truth, then I understand. You do what you feel that you have to do.

I just feel positive about our future. With the counselor and the AA meetings, I know that we can finally be that perfect couple that you always wanted us to be. I love you and our beautiful children. Give them a big kiss for me, baby. I want to hold you in my arms so bad, but I know I can't, not until I get the help I need.

Love, Mike

The tears came rolling down my face. He was trying to get some help to save our marriage. What should I do? If I testifed against him, then he would go to prison. But could I lie and say that he had only hit me once since we'd been married? What if the judge found out that I was lying and tried to take my kids from me? Mike, why are you putting me in this situation? I just didn't know what to do.

I tore up the letter so no one would ever see it. I just couldn't think about this right now. I decided to do some cleaning like I planned and maybe in a few days, I would decide what to do. The day went by fast. The sisters called and asked if I wanted to come over for dinner. They were great cooks and after missing a few meals that week, I found myself extremely hungry. I went over about six o'clock for dinner. Fried chicken, macaroni and cheese, green beans, hot buttered rolls, and chocolate cake for dessert. No wonder the kids loved it there so much.

After visiting with the kids for a couple of hours, I could tell they were getting sleepy. I gave them a bath and tucked them in for the night. The sisters wanted me to spend the night, but I had already imposed enough on their kindness. They walked me to the front door and watched me go into the house. The only thing I wanted to do was take a hot shower and go to bed.

I knew that I had gained at least five pounds that night. That food was so delicious.

When I walked into the bedroom and turned on the light, Mike was sitting on the bed. He darn near scared me half to death.

"Mike, what are you doing here?"

"Not so loud. I snuck in the back door so no one could see me. Baby, I missed you so much. I just had to come here and hold you in my arms."

Mike stood in front of me and put his hands on my face. I didn't know if I should stand there or try to run out the door. His hands felt so gentle. He walked closer to me and kissed me on my lips, the longest passionate kiss that I had ever received. He kissed my face and neck. It felt so good. He gently picked me up and laid me across the bed.

While standing in front of me, Mike took off his shirt and his pants. What was I doing? This was the same man that beat the hell out of me last week. But it wasn't the same man. It was someone different. He lay on the bed next to me, and pulled down the straps on my dress. Gently in my ear he whispered, "Sara, I love you."

As I closed my eyes, I could feel his tongue circling my nipples. The warmth of his hands was so soothing. My body ached to feel him inside me. For the first time in years, my husband and I made love. I woke up later that night, but Mike was gone. Was it a dream? Was he really here? I could tell by the wetness of the sheet, my husband had come home. I went back to sleep with a smile on my face. There was hope for my marriage.

Another week had gone by. It was definitely time for me to go back to work. The soreness and pain were completely gone. The bruises had faded from my face and my body. I felt much better, looking forward to my next visit from Mike. The trial was tomorrow. I was still a little skeptical, but I knew what I had to do to save the marriage and my family.

After my morning cup of brew, it was time for Michelle and me to face the Monday morning traffic. The neighbors were up early as usual. Michelle looked so pretty with her red ribbons in her hair. She was so excited that I was taking her to school. Michael Jr. was getting so big.

"Good morning, everyone."

"Good morning, Sara. Are you sure that you're ready to go back to work?"

"Yes ladies. I'm ready to be a mother again also. I'll pick up the kids clothes this evening when I get in from work. Are you ready to come home with me, big guy? I have missed them the last couple of weeks. Ladies, I feel like I just owe you so much. Are you sure that there's nothing I can do for the two of you?"

"Just letting us be a part of the children's lives is payment enough."

"Well, come on, Michelle, let's hit the road."

"Mommy."

"Yes, baby."

"Where's Daddy?"

"Mommy is going to tell you all about that later when you get home from school. But don't you worry, Daddy is just fine."

"Alright, Mommy. I love you."

"I love you too, baby."

Michelle got into the car and buckled her seatbelt. She was such a good little girl.

Just as I thought, Monday morning traffic never changes. It was still heavy as usual, with all of these young children out here on the road. Half of them were on cell phones, and the other half were busy texting one another. They just weren't paying enough attention to where they were going. It's a miracle that they make it to school without having an accident.

I dropped Michelle off safe and sound, and then it was my turn. Although I had been working this job for years, I couldn't help but feel butterflies in my stomach. It just seemed as though this was my first day at work for some reason. It was as if I was about to face some unknown challenge. When I drove into the parking lot, I noticed a red Mustang parked in back of the store. That car looks just like Mike's car, I thought. Just out of curiosity, I parked next to it. Oh my goodness, it was Mike's car.

I walked up to the driver's side. The window slowly let down halfway. A man's hand came out of the window and handed me an envelope. That definitely wasn't Mike's hand. It had to be Chris. The window was let up and the car backed out of the parking lot. I quickly walked into the back entrance of the shop. Trying desperately not to be seen, I unlocked the basement door and went downstairs. I opened the small white envelope. Inside was a one-page letter and five one hundred dollar bills.

Dear Sara,

I miss you so much. I can't stop thinking about a couple of weeks ago when we made love. I am still attending my AA meetings and seeing the counselor three times a week. I feel that I've made so much progress. The money, well, let's just say it's well overdue. I should have been helping you with the bills and the kids a long time ago. I truly intend to make up for all of that. That is, if you've decided to testify for me tomorrow. It's all up to you, baby. Like I said, I know that I'm asking you to lie for me, but I just feel like we can have the marriage that we both want if I'm able to continue to get the help I need. Chris said that Tom has been watching the house, that's why I got him to wait for you to come to work in order to give you this letter. Whatever you decide to do, just know that I love you and the kids very much.

All my love, Mike

It was clear as water what I had to do in that courtroom tomorrow. I knew I'd better get upstairs and let everyone know that I was there. Trying not to make too much noise, I took off my heels and walked down the hall. It was still a little early, so I figured everyone must be in the break room. As I approached the door, I heard women's voices.

"Lisa, isn't Sara due back today?"

"That's what Edna said. But Edna also said that she was out with the flu, and we all know that is a lie."

"Maybe she was out sick. Stop always assuming the worst."

"Shannon, please, you know as well as I do that Mike beat her up again. Everyone knows. She'll either stay at home until she's better, or she'll come to work wearing a face full of makeup to cover up the bruises."

"I feel sorry for her. Why doesn't she just leave that guy? She's pretty. She's smart. She doesn't need him. I'm sure she can find another man, maybe one that might even love her."

"She doesn't realize how lucky she is, Shannon. You know my sister Rachel."

"The one who just got out of the hospital?"

"Yes. Rachel and I were not only sisters, but we were best friends. When we were little, we used to pretend that we were twins. I was only two years younger than her, but we loved each other so much and looked so much alike. Everyone just assumed we were twins. Rachel got married to the man of her dreams about three years ago. He took her to Missouri to live in a house that he bought for her as a wedding present.

"Something just wasn't right about this guy. My grandmother told me once that anyone that did a lot of bragging about themselves was obviously a liar. I just didn't have a good feeling about Randy from day one. My mother just said that I was jealous because I was losing my sister. Rachel called me every day when she first got married. I asked her what happened to her honeymoon in the Bahamas. She said that Randy had business meetings that week and he couldn't get away. The calls went from daily to weekly to monthly, then not at all. She just stopped calling all together. I tried to call her several times, but Randy would answer the phone and say that Rachel was either at school or at work. My brother even tried to call in the middle of the night, but the answering machine picked up.

"This went on for about two years," she continued. "I called the school that Rachel was supposed to be attending. It was a culinary arts school. They had no records of a student by that name. Mother and I both got worried and decided to go and visit her in Missouri. When we arrived there, we passed by the bakery that Rachel said she worked at. I went in and asked the manager if Rachel was working. The manager said he didn't have anyone working there by that name. Mother started to cry. We both knew in our hearts that something was definitely wrong. Rachel loved her family. There was no way she would just stop all communication and lie about where she worked unless something had happened to her."

Lisa's voice broke, and then she went on with her story.

"We went to the house where they stayed. It was the worst-looking house on the street. It was old and ragged. The roof needed fixing. The grass hadn't been cut in at least a few months. There were no cars in the driveway. I asked the neighbors if they saw a young woman who looked like me. One of them said that they did see a pretty young woman there about a year ago, but all they see now is a young man going in and out. They just assumed that the woman left because the young man wouldn't keep up the place and pay the rent.

"Rachel told us that Randy had bought her a house. She didn't mention anything about rent. We walked around to the back door. Randy must have been in a big hurry to leave. He forgot to lock the door. I called the police from my cell phone. We waited for them to arrive before entering the house. We explained that Rachel was living there, but she was missing. The house looked and smelled terrible. There were dishes stacked in the sink. No one had washed them in several days. Everything was dusty and filthy.

"The police searched the house," she continued. "They found Rachel's clothes in the bedroom. There were red stains on the floor. The officer said it could possibly be blood. They followed the stains to a locked door in the back of the house. When they broke the handle off, the door immediately opened. It was a basement. A stinking one at that. There was a small amount of light at the end of the stairs. I called out

Rachel's name. The police went down the stairs and found her lying on an old mattress in the corner. She was so weak. She had this blank stare in her face. We took her to the hospital.

"Randy had been keeping her locked in the basement for two years," Lisa said. "He had been beating on her, making her lie to her family and friends. One day she tried to escape when he went to work. But one of his buddies who worked with him at the auto body shop called and told him that they saw Rachel running down the street. He caught her before she could get anywhere and took her back to that house. He kept her locked up so she couldn't get away from him. They put his ass in prison, but he screwed up Rachel's mind real bad. She stayed in that mental institution for a year."

"Lisa, I am so sorry, girl. Why didn't you ever tell me this before? I knew she was shy, and your parents wanted her to live with them, but I just figured they wanted to take care of her."

"She's getting better. At least she's not having any more nightmares about what happened. The doctor said hopefully in a few months she should be back to her normal self. I don't think she will ever be normal again. Rachel will forever carry around those scars in her heart. That's why Sara makes me sick. She has a chance to get out. My sister tried to get out and couldn't. What is wrong with woman like her? They are sick."

I walked into the break room. Lisa was sitting at the table crying. Shannon was standing next to her rubbing Lisa's back. Shannon glanced up and looked me straight in the face.

"Sara. Welcome back. I hope that you're feeling better. Lisa and I were just talking about a family situation. We were just on our way back to work."

Lisa walked by me, cleaning her face with a napkin. She didn't even look at me. Lisa's story freaked me out. I felt so bad for her. But Lisa was wrong; my situation had nothing to do with her sister's. Mike would never do all those things to me. He was gonna get better.

"Sara, is that you, girl?"

"Hi, Edna."

"Come over here and give me a hug. Sara, I've missed you so much. I am so glad you're back to work. Do you feel alright?"

"I'm just fine, Edna. Thank you and Joe for the flowers and everything that you all did for me and the kids."

"You don't have to thank me, baby. We're family. We have to take care of each other."

Edna and I hugged each other and we both went to work. The entire week was hectic. I hadn't seen that many people there since the holidays. Business was so good. I was getting overtime even when I didn't want overtime.

CHAPTER TWENTY-TWO:

The Trial

The day of trial finally came. I took Michelle to school and then I went to the courthouse. I sat there for an hour before Mike's case finally came up. He looked so handsome sitting there with his suit on. I was nervous, but I knew what I had to do. They called me to the stand, and the lawyer immediately asked me what happened that night when I went to the hospital. I did exactly what Mike asked me to do. When the lawyer asked if this was the first time that Mike had ever hit me, I told him that Mike didn't hit me, he slapped me. That's when I accidentally fell down to the floor. It was the first time that he ever slapped me, I said.

Tom was in the courtroom sitting in the back. After I testified, he got up and walked out. Tom must have had a feeling about what I was about to do; I guess that's why he didn't tell Mama about the date of the trial. The court dropped the charges against Mike. I got a chance to talk to him briefly after the trial.

"Mike. How are you doing?"

"I'm doing great, Sara." He held my hands. "I'm sorry that I put you through all of that. I'll never ask you to lie like that again."

"When are you coming home?"

"Not right now. I want to come home when I feel like I can be a husband to you and a father to our children. Give me a few more months to get myself together. I'll come by the house this weekend to see you and the kids. Is that alright with you?"

"Yes, it's alright with me. Mike, I love you,"

"I love you too. I better get out of here, before these guys decide to lock me up anyway. I'll see you this weekend."

He kissed me on the cheek and walked away with Chris. I had to leave to get to work.

It was Saturday morning. The kids and I were excited because Mike was coming to visit. We decided to have a welcome home party. We had cake, ice cream, and pizza. We waited the entire day and night, but Mike never showed up. Sunday morning came. I just knew he would come by that day. He still didn't show up. The kids and I finally ate the food we got for Mike's welcome home party. I thought maybe he decided to come by after the kids went to bed, but when I woke up Monday morning, there was no sign of Mike.

The only explanation that I had for Michelle was that maybe I misunderstood what he said. Maybe he would come by the next weekend. I got her a new outfit and a beginner's computer. She was excited and forgot all about Mike.

Six months went by. Things were pretty good. Chris would still show up at the house with envelopes of money and letters from Mike. They all stated that he was doing fine and he was almost ready to come home. So much had happened since the last time I saw him. Michael Jr. was walking. He had skipped the crawling phase and went straight into walking. I took the kids to visit everyone in Loxley just about every other weekend. They loved it there. Mama was still happy to hear that Mike hadn't moved back into the house. I told her I didn't think he would ever come home.

Janie was happy. She was seven months pregnant. All she talked about was her baby girl. Rex fixed up one of the rooms for the baby. It was absolutely beautiful. I think they had every piece of baby furniture you could think of in that room. The walls and ceiling were painted baby blue with white clouds and a colorful rainbow. Different kinds of birds and butterflies were drawn on the wall. It was absolutely gorgeous.

Tom and I finally ran into each other and had that long-awaited conversation that he had been putting off. "Hello, Tom."

"Sara. How are you and the children doing?"

"We're just fine. Tom, I want to thank you for not saying anything to Mama about the trial. I only did what I did because of Mike. He's doing so much better now. There is no way he would have gotten the help he needed behind bars. He is the one who refuses to come back home. He wants to get better first, and I think he will."

"I hope for your sake that you're right. I didn't tell your mama what happened at the trial because it would have hurt her to know that her daughter lied under oath in a court of law, defending a man that has done nothing but cause her pain. I just don't feel like Mike is going to ever change, but like I said, I hope for the sake of you and your children that I'm wrong."

Tom and I didn't speak anymore that day.

That evening when the kids and I got back to the house, I saw Mike's car parked in the driveway. "Mommy, is Daddy home?"

"I think so, Michelle. Let's go inside and see if he's here."

By the time I got Michael Jr. out of his car seat, the front door opened. It was Mike. He had finally come home to stay. I was so happy to see him. Michelle hugged him, but I'm not sure if she cared whether he was there or not. Michael Jr. did allow Mike to pick him up without crying this time.

Everything seemed to be going along well for the next few months, but after that, I felt things were slowly going back to the way they were. Although Mike wasn't hitting me, we still never got a chance to spend much time together. He stopped giving me money for the bills or the kids. Mike still worked all night, coming home in the mornings. Some mornings he didn't even bother to come home. He'd be gone for days at a time. He stayed home on Sundays and took the children to the park.

Michelle usually liked to go to the park, but the last time he took her and Michael Jr., she told me that she didn't want to go back there anymore. "Mommy, do I have to go to the park with Daddy on Sundays?"

"Michelle, I thought you enjoyed going to the park."

"I do, but I don't want to go with Daddy anymore."

"Why not? What happened, Michelle?"

"He always takes that strange man with us. He's tall and his eyes are scary. All they do is sit there and whisper in each other's ear."

"What! Chris, the tall man with blonde hair and hazel eyes? Cat's eyes."

"Yeah, that sounds like him. He's creepy looking. They sit there and talk while I play with Michael Jr. It's not fun anymore, not like it is when you take us. Do we have to go back there with him?"

"No, baby, you don't have to go back there with him. We'll find something else for you to do."

"Thank you, Mommy."

When I questioned Mike about what goes on at the park with the children, I could feel that same anger inside him. "How are things going at the park with the kids, honey?"

"What do you mean, how are things going at the park with the kids? Is there a problem with me taking my own kids to the damn park?"

"No, not at all."

"Because if there is a problem, then you can take them yourself!"

"Well, Michelle wants to start spending the night with some of her friends on the weekends. I told her that it sounded like a good idea for her to visit with other kids her own age. Michael Jr. can find something to keep himself occupied, so that way you don't have to worry about the Sunday park visits."

"First you tell me I don't spend enough time with the kids, and then when I try to spend time with them, you tell me they don't want to spend time with me. So let's just forget it. I can go to work on Sundays. I need the extra money anyway."

"Speaking of extra money, Mike, it's been a few months since you've given me any money for anything."

"That's all you women want. You make a paycheck of your own, but you still want every dime that a man has."

"I didn't mean it like that. You promised when you came home, you would finally help out more."

He reached into his pocket and pulled out a twenty-dollar bill.

"Here you go, sweetie," he said as he threw the money onto the floor. "I'm going to have a drink, before I do something that we might both regret."

Mike walked out the front door and slammed it behind him. A drink? He told me that he had been attending AA meetings and he wasn't drinking anymore. That liar. How could he have made all those promises to me? They were all just a pack of lies. You did it again, Sara, falling again for his crap."

CHAPTER TWENTY-THREE:

The Real Mike Is Back

Two years went by. Everything was pretty much the same. Mike did his thing and I did mine. We barely even saw each other. At least the beatings had stopped. He'd come home from work while I was on my way out the door to work. Most of the time, he'd be gone in the afternoons when I got back to the house. The kids didn't miss him. Michael Jr. never really got a chance to know him as a father anyway, and Michelle had more respect for Rex and Tom than she had for her own father.

The kids and I spent a lot of time at the neighbors' house. Ms. Abigail had been feeling poorly. I remembered all those years that she helped me and the kids, so I wanted to be there for her. She was pretty weak, but she was convinced that she would be as good as new. The Peck sisters were getting older and didn't want to face the fact. But I would always be there for them because I owed them both at least that much. Michael Jr. was turning three years old on Friday. We had planned a small party for him at one of the local pizza places. That boy loved pizza. He liked going there to play the games and seeing all the different characters they had to entertain the children. Mama had also planned a party for him at the farm the following weekend. Michael Jr. was a special little boy. Some children couldn't even have one birthday party; he was about to have two. I asked Mike if he could attend his son's party. He told me that he would think about it. Nevertheless, the party was going to take place whether he was there or not.

The weekend finally came. The family came down from Loxley to attend Michael Jr.'s birthday party. We all had a great time, with balloons, games, clowns, lots of pizza, and a huge birthday cake. Michael Jr. had such a good time. Janie brought her beautiful baby girl. She named her Julia Cheyenne, after our mother. The party lasted for at least four hours, but Mike never showed up. I guess it was a good thing that he didn't. That day was so perfect. All of the kids were tired at the end of the day. Michael Jr. fell asleep as soon as I got him into the car.

By the time, I drove into the driveway, I could tell that Mike had been there. He left every light on in the house. Mike left a red tricycle in the living room. A big red bow was tied to the handlebars, along with the price tag.

"Michael Jr., come here, baby, look what Daddy left for you. Daddy got you a tricycle for your birthday." MJ looked at the tricycle, but when I asked him to get on, he started to cry. "Come on, baby. Put your foot on the pedal."

Michael Jr. started to cry louder and louder.

"Mommy, please, make him stop," Michelle said as she put her hands over her ears.

"Come on, honey. You don't have to ride it. It's OK."

I picked him up and held him in my arms and all of a sudden he stopped crying. When I put him down on the floor next to the tricycle, he started to cry again. He constantly kept looking at that tricycle as if he were afraid of it.

"Michelle, watch your brother for a minute."

I took the tricycle out on the back porch. "OK…Mama's little man. It's gone. It won't hurt you, OK?"

"OK, Mama."

"That's my little man. Come on. Mama's gonna get you ready for bed. You had so much fun today and you were such a good little boy. I love you."

"I love you, Mama," Michael Jr. replied.

The next day, since my wonderful husband left the price tag on the tricycle, I was able to take it back to the store and exchange it for a different one. I got him a dark blue one with a toy horn on the handlebars. Michael Jr. loved it. He rode his new tricycle just about every day outside.

Mike drove up in the driveway one Saturday morning. Michael Jr. was riding his tricycle on the driveway. When Mike got out of his car, Michael Jr. immediately started blowing his toy horn.

"Hey, little man, you're blowing that horn as if you didn't want me to park in my own driveway."

Michael Jr. didn't say a word. He just sat on his tricycle looking at Mike, continuing to blow his toy horn.

"I'll tell you what, MJ, let me go inside and put my things down, and I'll come back out and park my car on the street in front of the house behind Mama's car. The driveway will be all yours."

Michael Jr. stopped blowing his horn as if that's exactly what he wanted Mike to do all along.

"Wait a minute; this ain't the tricycle I bought you. I know it didn't have that loud-ass horn on the handlebars. Who got you this tricycle?" When Mike touched the tricycle, Michael Jr. rode down the driveway toward the street. "Hey! Get back here, little boy. MJ, don't go into the street."

As soon as I heard Mike's voice, I dropped the laundry onto the floor and ran outside to see what was going on. Mike ran toward the street behind Michael Jr.

"Come back here, you little idiot!" A car was coming down the street. I could see it from the porch. When Michael Jr. got to the edge of the driveway, he stopped his tricycle. Mike was running so fast, he couldn't stop. He ended up in the middle of the street. I screamed because I just knew Mike was going to be hit by that car. Thank goodness it was Mr. Howard, an elderly gentleman who lived a few houses down the road. When he saw Mike, he immediately jammed on his brakes, stopping his car. Mike was terrified.

Once he caught his breath, he looked over at Michael Jr. sitting on his tricycle. For some strange reason, Michael Jr. had a huge smile on his face as he began to blow his little horn again. Mike grabbed his belongings that he had dropped on the ground and ran toward the front porch. He didn't say a word; he just stood in front of me. I did notice that there was a huge wet spot on the front of his pants. That brought back memories. I remembered one day when Mike was driving his car behind me and Timmy as we were running home from school. Oh, how I begged him to stop, but he wouldn't. I remembered looking over at Timmy and noticing that he had urinated in his pants, just like Mike did today. Funny how the old saying states, "What goes around, comes back around."

This would have been the best day of Timmy's life. I must tell him one day. Mike walked past me into the house. Michael Jr. turned his tricycle around and rode back toward the house. "Sweetie, don't go into the street. Alright?"

"Yes, Mama," Michael Jr. replied as he continued to play as if nothing ever happened. Somehow I felt that I should be angry with him, or even punish him. "I love you, baby. As soon as Mama is finished with the laundry, we're gonna go to the park."

"Yes, yes, the park, Mama."

"OK, baby, stay on the driveway."

As I walked into the house, Mike was standing behind me in the living room. Slowly walking toward me, he asked, "Whose kid is that?"

"Mike, are you alright? You should go into the bedroom and change your pants. I don't know if you've noticed or not, but they are wet."

"You heard me, Sara, whose kid is that? I want a DNA test done."

I just stood there looking totally in shock. "Where is this coming from?"

"That is the son of the devil sitting out there on that tricycle. That kid just tried to kill me, and you saw it."

"Mike, he didn't know that you were going to run into the street. MJ rides his tricycle all the time on the driveway. He never goes into the street. Never!"

"What happened to the tricycle I bought him?"

"He didn't like it, so I got him a different color."

Mike started to mimic the words I just said. "He didn't like it, so I got him a different color. Since when do you let these kids tell you what the hell to do?" Mike started knocking things onto the floor.

"Mike, maybe if you would spend some time with MJ and try to bond with him, he would react to you a little differently. When was the last time you told either of your kids that you love them? Better yet, when is the last time you hugged or kissed one of them?"

"Don't throw that crap at me. I spent time with those kids. I took them to the park."

"Yeah, but you didn't play with them or spend time with them. All you did was sit there and talk to Chris."

"Chris? Who told you that?" Mike grabbed my neck with his hand. "I said, who told you that? Oh...I know. It was one of those little demon seeds of yours. Michelle. That's who it was. What else did she tell you?"

That same old look of rage and anger was in his eyes. I could tell he wanted to hit me. It's as if he was turning into that same old monster again. Mike glanced up and saw Michael Jr. standing at the front door. Mike had dropped his wallet outside. MJ picked it up and brought it into the house. He threw it on the living room floor. Mike let go of my neck immediately and slowly walked over and picked up his wallet. "I'm out of here."

Mike waited for Michael Jr. to step away from the front door before he went outside.

We heard Mike's car cranking up. Just afterward, there was a loud crash. Mike drove off down the street. I ran out the front door to see what was going on. Mike had purposely run over Michael Jr.'s tricycle in the driveway. I grabbed MJ because

I didn't want him to come outside and see what kind of monster he had for a father.

"Baby, you look so tired. Why don't you take a nap for a while, and then when you wake up, Mommy will take you to Ms. Abigail's house for a chocolate brownie with nuts. We can go by and pick up Michelle from Aunt Edna's house and then come back home."

"What about the park, Mommy?"

"Well, your tricycle has a flat tire, so you can't ride it in the park like we had planned."

"I want to go to the park and swing."

"OK, we can go and swing."

"Yes. Yes."

MJ was so excited. He just wanted to go to the park. He didn't care if he rode his tricycle or not. He immediately ran to his bedroom and lay down on his bed. That gave me time to go back outside and throw that definitely not repairable tricycle into the Dumpster down the street. "I hate Mike Farraday."

Oh my goodness, did I say that out loud? Michael Jr. scared him to death. If it had not been for my little boy today, there's no telling how bad Mike would have beaten me. All of the AA meetings and counseling is not helping him at all.

What was the deal with him and Chris? He spent more time with him than his own family. It didn't matter anymore. I was tired of all the different changes. I wanted my kids to grow up in a stable, happy, loving environment, and it just wasn't going to happen at that house. Mike just wasn't getting any better. It had been eight years. I wasn't even thirty and I felt like I was eighty.

At that point, I decided to save my paychecks and buy only what the kids and I needed. As soon as Michelle finished this school year, we were out of here. We would move back to Loxley. That's where I should have stayed in the beginning. I just needed to hang in here eight more months. By then, Michelle would be in the fourth grade and Michael Jr. would be four years old. I hated to leave my home and my new friends, but

I had to think about my children's happiness for the first time in my life. I needed to do what was best for them. Every day I could feel myself disliking Mike more and more and more.

I wasn't going to tell anyone my plans, not even my own mama. I didn't want Mike to ever suspect that I was leaving and taking the kids. Who knows, he might be happy as can be, but then again he might make a big deal out of it and try to beat me just for the hell of it. I just didn't want to go there with him until I had to.

CHAPTER TWENTY-FOUR:

I Know What I Have to Do

The next few weeks went by fast. Everything was pretty peaceful. Lisa and I finally started talking to each other again at work. That made me happy. I was sitting in my office busy as usual when I heard a soft knock at my door. As I glanced up, I noticed Lisa standing in the doorway.

"Ms. Edna said you wanted to see me, Sara."

"Yes, I do. Come in and have a seat."

"Sara, I know I said some cruel things to you a while back. I want to apologize. It's not my place to cast judgment on you. I'm ashamed of myself for feeling that way."

"I accept your apology, but you don't have anything to apologize for. I am weak and naive just like everybody says I am. I believed everything that Mike told me and I believed it because I wanted to. I've spent the last ten years of my life pretending. Playing house, pretending that I had the perfect husband, and it's all just a bunch of lies. Lisa, I am so sorry about what happened to your sister. I'd like to talk to her someday and try to get to know her. Trust me, I have been a prisoner. My mind has been locked up for years. My sense of reasoning and priorities was chained up for a long time, but all of that is about to change."

"Are you leaving Mike?"

"If I ever leave the shop, I'm gonna ask Edna to give you my position as assistant manager."

"Sara...Are you serious?" Lisa asked with tears in her eyes. 'I don't want to take your position. You can't leave the shop. If it hadn't been for you, this shop wouldn't have advanced the way it has. We all owe our jobs to you. Business is wonderful and it's all because of you."

Lisa was crying hard now. "Sara, I'm sorry. I'm being so selfish. You do what you have to do, and if leaving Henderson is the answer, then you do just that. I'll be proud to fill your shoes one day."

"Thank you, and I'd appreciate it if you didn't tell anyone about our conversation, especially Edna or Shannon. I'm just gonna be honest with you: I know at times you like to gossip, but I'm begging you to please keep all of this that I am saying to you today to yourself. This is just something that I was thinking about doing maybe in the future. I'm still not sure. This is a big step for me. I mean, who knows, I'll probably just stay here and just keep working. You guys have really criticized my life. Now, I'm not saying that I didn't deserve it, but what I am saying is that it doesn't feel good. It hurts to walk into a room only to find out that you are the topic of conversation and not in a good way."

"Sara, you're a good woman. I know that I am the main one who has been guilty of the gossip, and the criticizing, but it was never about you. I had to talk to someone. You wouldn't listen to me. I just don't want to see you go down the path that so many battered women go down. You have been stuck in denial for years. You thought that your marriage was going to be perfect one day. It's just not going to happen, not with Mike Farraday. But if you get some help for yourself and figure out what made you stay there for so many years, then maybe one day you can find that perfect man. It is possible you know?"

We both started to laugh. Lisa gave me a big hug. Tears were flowing everywhere in that office. At that moment, I still wasn't sure what I had to do, but I knew that my children had to be the first priority in my life. Lisa and I never spoke about the conversation we had that day. Work was good. Lisa endured some long hours proving that if the time came, she could definitely handle the assistant manager's position.

A couple of months later, a tall brunette with long curly hair approached me as I was grocery shopping one evening. As she got closer to me, I noticed she was wearing sunglasses.

"Are you Mike Farraday's wife?"

I was almost afraid to answer her. "Yes, I'm Mike's wife. Who are you?"

"My name is Tina. I'm a dancer at Big Billy's Lounge. Your husband works there. You've got to get away from him."

"What are you talking about? What did you say your name was again?"

"My name is Tina, and I'm talking about your husband, Mike."

She pulled off her sunglasses. Oh my goodness. She had a terrible black eye. The left side of her face was swollen and bruised. She lifted up the right side of her shirt, and her back and stomach were covered with black and blue bruises.

"That crazy bastard beat me up last night in the dressing room. He hit me in the face with his gun. He wants me to quit. Mike says I'm too old to work there as a stripper. Girl, I'm only thirty-four years old. They've got this plan to bring in sixteen- and eighteen-year-old girls to replace us."

"Those are children. Mike knows they can't allow anyone to work in a club unless they are twenty-one years old."

"No, honey. These ain't your average girl-next-door-looking sixteen-year-olds. These whores look like they've been turning tricks for years. Ain't nobody gonna ask them for an ID, trust me."

"Mike has a gun?"

"Yes, he has one. Along with everyone else that works at the club. He beat me so bad, then his boy toy Chris threw me out into the alley. They didn't care if I lived or died."

"Chris."

"You don't know about those two, do you? Girlfriend, get away from that husband of yours, he's just using you for look purposes only. He's never gonna stop beating on you, baby. Never! He is sick. You don't know half of what he's capable of. Get away from him while you can, because when my old man gets out of prison, Mike Farraday is as good as dead. He's only got a few more months to do in the state pen, and then he's coming home. He's not gonna like what I have to say about Mike and Chris, so I suggest you get your kids and take the high road, sister, as soon as possible."

I didn't know what to make of any of this conversation. I was totally baffled by everything I had just heard.

Tina grabbed my arm and whispered in my ear, "For your sake, it would be best if you didn't tell anyone about our little conversation today. I'm not threatening you, I'm trying to help you, girl. Please get away from that fool before it's too late."

Tina let go of my arm and put on her sunglasses. We both looked to see if anyone was coming down the aisle. When I looked around, Tina was gone. She disappeared almost into thin air. Strangely enough, I believed her story. Mike was definitely a sick man. The only way he felt in control of a situation was by hitting on a woman. That made him feel like Mr. Michael Farraday, a real man. Sara, you better get out of here and go pick up your kids before another strange woman comes up to you, I told myself.

"Mrs. Farraday. Mrs. Farraday. Are you ready to check out? Sara, did you hear me? I can check you out at register two."

"I'm sorry, Debbie. My head was somewhere else. Did you see a tall brunette with long curly hair wearing shades earlier in the store?"

"No. I didn't see her."

As I got home later that evening, I still couldn't get Tina's face out of my mind. Although she was in pain, she still wore a vengeful smile on her red lips. It was as if she had already tasted the future and it was sweet. The bruises and the raccoon eye reminded me so much of my own war that I had been facing for the past eight years. Even though she had been beaten, I could still tell that she was a beautiful woman. Her hair was long and filled with curls that had the look of silk.

I tried to sleep in my bed. While I tossed and turned, the conversation we had just kept playing over and over again like a broken record. I could still hear her voice as if she were in the room. What did she mean by Chris being Mike's boy toy? Sometimes I wish that I would have been raised in the city instead of on a farm. I just didn't understand so many things. Was she going to get her husband to kill Mike when he got out of jail? What about my kids?

After closing my eyes for what seemed to be a brief minute, the alarm clock started to buzz.

"Come on, you've got to be kidding. It's six o'clock and I haven't slept all night. Damn it! Oh well. This is not going to be one of my best days. Come on, girl, roll out of bed and let's get this show on the road."

CHAPTER TWENTY-FIVE:

Preparing for the Trip Back to Loxley

The days were long and the nights were short. I was tired, but I had to do what I had to do. Every payday I sent Janie some money. I had her open a checking account in Loxley for me in her name. Until I decided just what I wanted to do, I couldn't take any chances on Mike suspecting anything, or I may have to kill him myself.

I had worked ten-hour shifts that whole week. At least nine of them had to have been spent on my feet each day. I wanted to rest this weekend, but I had promised the kids I'd take them to the church bazaar. Mike came home that Sunday morning. The children and I were just about to go and meet Edna and Joe at the church. He tried his best to start an argument, but I wasn't about to fall for his game.

"Sara, where are you going this morning?" He stood in front of the doorway blocking our exit.

"I'm taking the kids to church this morning."

"Where's my breakfast?"

"I didn't know you were coming home, so I didn't cook anything for you, but there is some fried chicken, lasagna, and peach cobbler in the refrigerator. All you have to do is heat it up in the microwave. We'll be back later. I'll bring you a plate from the church."

"Whatever happened to those days when you prepared my meals and had them ready for me on the stove? The little wife doesn't do that anymore?"

"The kids and I are in a big hurry. They're having a youth day program for the children at the church. They are excited about being involved. Why don't you get some rest?"

"How would you like to go to church with a bloody nose, Sara Farraday?" He stood there in the doorway laughing.

"Mommy, can we please go?" Michelle asked. "Daddy, please let us go. We're gonna be late."

"Oh...Michelle wants to go to church. How cute. Is your little boyfriend gonna be there? What's his name? That kid from down the street, Peter. He's gonna be at church too, isn't he? I better not find out that you been fooling around with that kid or—"

"Mike! Stop it! She's just eight years old."

"Well, she looks a lot older than eight."

Michael Jr. was anxious to go. He started crying.

"Oh, please!" Mike said. "Take that little demon to church. Maybe it can help him. Go on, get out of here."

Mike walked into the house and we quickly went out the front door to the car. I hated for the kids to go through all of that, but soon it would come to an end one way or another.

Once we finally got to church, the kids had a great time. They participated in the Bible stories and plays. The church served a huge dinner afterward, with chicken, hot dogs, hamburgers, potato salad, macaroni, pasta salad, cakes, pies—tons of food. There were games, toys, singing; everyone of all ages was overcome with excitement. I tried to stay at the church with the kids as long as I could, in my attempt to avoid Mike. I didn't want anymore run-ins with Mr. Farraday today.

"The kids are having a good time today," Edna said.

"Yes, they are. Thank you so much for inviting us. I know we haven't been attending church often and I blame myself for that. Mike told me the only day he could spend time with the kids was on Sundays. That turned out to be a big mistake."

"You tried. Mike is a bitter and angry person. He's always been that way since his granddaddy died. Well, I mean, his daddy. Tom told me that you overheard him and Mike talking that day at the house and you know that he had been pretending to be Mike's father. The only problem is, we didn't know Mike had known all these years and was just pretending not to know. But I guess it all makes sense now.

"I remember the day of Daddy's funeral," Edna said. "Mike told us that he wasn't going. We left him at the house. He was so angry, because his grandfather died and left him here on this earth alone. But somehow, he had to have shown up and overheard Joe, Tom, and myself talking. That's the only way he would have known that Tom was sterile and Daddy had sex with his mother. He's always been a sneaky little devil. Even as a baby, he never bonded with anyone but Daddy. He loved that old man. I think his death did a lot more to Mike's head than he's willing to admit. I'm just glad that things are working out better between the two of you and he's finally seeing a counselor."

"Edna, I lied. Things aren't better between Mike and me."

"But I thought he had left the house and was attending the AA meetings and getting counseling. I haven't seen any bruises on your face since he's been back home. I just assumed everything was better."

"He hasn't been beating me as bad as he used to. It seems as though every time he grabs me, Michael Jr. starts to cry or scream out. You know yourself that I can do magic to this face with makeup. Edna, I lied to the judge in court."

"You didn't tell anyone else, did you?"

"No. I told the judge that Mike had only hit me once and that's when I accidentally fell on the floor and broke my ribs. He told me that he could get more help attending AA meetings and going to counseling than being locked up behind bars in a jail. Yes, I believed him."

"You committed a crime. Do you know that you could have gone to jail? Do you know that the judge could have taken away your kids? Sara, I love my nephew, but I'm not about to lie for him. No, ma'am! He's not worth me going to jail over."

I couldn't help but cry.

"What about the AA meetings and the counseling?" she asked.

"He still smells like alcohol. I'm not sure if he ever saw a counselor or if he only said that just for me to testify to keep him from going to jail."

As I glanced up, I saw the kids running toward Edna and myself. "Mommy, Mommy, I'm tired. Why are your eyes so red, Mommy? Have you been crying?"

"No. It's just my allergies acting up again. You mean to tell me that Michelle is tired? Alright, baby. Get your little brother and let's get ready to go."

"You're leaving already?" Edna asked.

"Yes, the kids have school tomorrow. I better get them home so they can take a bath and get to bed early. Thank you again for inviting us. The kids and I had a wonderful time. Michael Jr., you look so sleepy. Come here, baby. Let's go to the car. Good-bye, Joe. See you tomorrow, Edna."

I loaded the kids up in the car. Boy, were they tired. They dozed off as we took the scenic route. I was dreading the ride home, not knowing what to expect once I got there, hoping that pretty little candy-apple-red Mustang wouldn't be in the driveway. As I drove up in the front yard, thank goodness, Mike's car was gone—but that didn't last long.

By the time I got the kids in the house and ready for bed, Mike was walking in the front door. Remember, Sara, stay calm. "Oh, you're back, missy."

"Mike, I brought you a plate from the church bizarre."

"Well, thank you, but I'm not hungry for food."

Mike walked over to me and grabbed my face.

"Since the little ones are in bed, why don't we go into our bedroom, sweetie, and have some alone time?" He started kissing my face and lips.

"But, honey, don't you want something to eat? I brought you all of that food."

"Yeah, I want to eat you. Now come on."

He pulled me into the bedroom. All of a sudden, I heard a loud noise coming from the children's room. Michael Jr. started crying.

"Mike. Mike. Let go of me. I need to go and check on the children."

"Damn you and those children!" Mike pushed my face away. "Go check on those little monsters of yours."

I quickly ran into the kids' room. Michelle's roller skates had dropped off her dresser onto the floor and startled MJ. He woke up crying because he was afraid.

"Hush, my little baby. It's alright. The skates fell on the floor, that's all. Mommy's here, baby."

I sat in the kids' room even after MJ had fallen asleep, hoping that Mike would also do the same. A couple of hours later, thank goodness, Mike was down for the count. I lay on the sofa. No way was I about to disturb him.

The sun was bright, shining through the window the next morning. When I finally opened my eyes, it dawned on me that I had slept on the sofa all night. Exhausted by the festivities, I didn't even hear Mike leaving to go to work. Between working long evenings at the shop and taking care of the kids, I was just totally worn out. Trying to send money home to Janie to put into the account she had opened for me was hard, but I had come too far to stop now.

It was time for the usual morning routine: shower, make breakfast, get the kids up and dressed, feed them, and head out the door. The sky was gray and cloudy. All of my old war wounds from Mike were sore today. I had a feeling it was gonna be a rainy day. I rushed to get the kids to school, just in time before the skies opened up and the liquid sunshine came pouring out. Nevertheless, it was still another workday.

I hadn't seen much of Mike for the past couple of weeks, until one morning about three o'clock. I was sleeping comfortably. I didn't know if I was dreaming or awake. Mike came home from work early again that morning. I just assumed he came home for sex as usual, but he wanted to talk instead.

"Sara, Sara."

"What do you want me to do, Mike?" I asked, feeling extremely groggy.

"Did you talk to a woman by the name of Tina?" Still half asleep, I couldn't even think straight. Tina. I figured he already knew the truth, so no since in lying to him.

"Yeah, some crazy woman came up to me in the grocery store one day. She said her name was Tina."

"Why didn't you tell me about her?"

"Mike, her eyes were red and she smelled like alcohol. I just figured she was some drunk or drug addict out of her mind. I don't even remember what she said. That's why I didn't mention it to you, honey."

"Are you sure, Sara?"

"Yes, I'm sure. I had forgotten all about it, baby."

"Did she say anything else, Sara?" I could tell Mike was getting a little aggravated with me.

"She told me she was a stripper at Big Billy's Lounge. I didn't see her face because she was wearing sunglasses. She also mentioned something about being tired of Henderson and she was leaving town. That's when I walked off and left her standing there. I thought she was going to beg for money or something."

"She didn't mention anything about me or Chris?"

"No."

"Very good."

I felt something stabbing into the side of my body. When I looked down, I was the one in for a surprise. "Mike, is that a gun in your belt?"

"Yes."

"What are you doing with a gun? Is your job that dangerous?"

"It's not just the job. When you start making a little money in this town, people have a tendency to get a little jealous of you."

"So, is it more for your personal protection?"

"Sara, you worry too much. Plus I need this gun for work. I meet up with some real live hotheads at times. This is my girl. She's always got my back. Trust me, it's more or less part of my uniform, babe. A nice piece of warm steel. See how nice she feels."

Mike took his gun and rubbed it slowly on my face. He went down the top of my nightgown, rubbing it between my breasts. "See how warm it is. That feels good, doesn't it, babe?"

"Mike, please stop."

"I'm not gonna hurt you. Besides, if I wanted to kill you, I could have shot you a long time ago. Sara, you've never lied to me before, have you?"

"No. Why would you ask me something like that?"

"You've been acting nervous and tense lately, like something is going on. Is there something going on that I should know about?"

"No. I'm just sleepy, and I have to get up and go to work in a few hours, that's all."

"Sara, you remember when we were in high school. My friends used to wonder why I was hanging around ugly Sara Ramsey. I told them you were not that ugly. OK, so you weren't a Sharon Howser or Rachel Miller or Summer Davis, but at least you were a real virgin the first time we had sex. I must say, girl, you were a good piece of ass. All those other girls were having sex with the football team, the basketball team, the soccer team. You name it, and they had sex with it. They were real live whores, but not you. You were special.

"I knew one day you would always belong to me," he said. "You would do anything I told you to do. That's what I love about you, Sara, loyal to the end. You grew up to be a fine-looking woman, Sara Ramsey. Nice long brown hair. Those big thighs of yours turn me on. Round, firm breasts with those big pink nipples."

Mike took the gun and put it under my nightgown. He rubbed my thighs slowly as he went higher and higher until I could feel the tip of his gun touching the crotch of my panties. I wanted to tell him to stop so badly, but I was afraid of what he might do if he became angry. Tears rolled down my face. With my eyes closed, lying in bed, I just hoped that whatever Mike had in store for me would be over soon. Mike's cell phone started to ring.

"Who the hell? What does he want? What's up? Yes, I'm on my way back to the club. No, we are not having sex. I said we are not having sex! Look, babe, I'll be back in fifteen minutes."

He hung up his phone. I still lay there and kept my eyes closed. "I've got to get back to work. Darn, I wanted to have sex with you, girl."

I kept my eyes closed as tightly as possible, not opening them until I heard Mike walking out the front door.

"Damn him. I hate him so much sometimes."

Growing up without a father is a feeling that I never wanted my children to experience. So desperately, I struggled to give them that sense of security that comes with a two-parent household. Now, I wondered if keeping them in this situation was more of a punishment than an act of love.

Time flew by fast. My hardest job wasn't working late hours; it was attempting to avoid Mike and praying that he wouldn't make any late-night rendezvous for the next few weeks. I really didn't want to leave Mike, but I couldn't turn him into the man that I wanted him to be. All I ever wanted was an unconditional love in my life. Some days he can be the sweetest person in the world, but other days he acts as if he could beat my brains out. How could I love someone who treated me so badly?

For the sake of my children, I had to get them out of the mess that I created. I hated even the idea of something happening to one of my kids because I was too stupid to get out of a bad relationship. All my dreams and fantasies—that's all they ever were—floated around in my imagination.

CHAPTER TWENTY-SIX:

How Much More Can I Take?

I called Janie one morning from work. I wanted to know if Rex could come by the house one night after Mike went to work and pick up the children's things. Mike never went into their room anyway, so he wouldn't notice that anything was missing.

"Hi, Janie."

"Hey, little sister."

"Look, I don't have much time to talk."

"You haven't changed your mind, have you?"

"Janie, this is the hardest decision I have ever had to make. I'm not stupid. I know that my children's safety is the most important thing."

"You have to set an example for your daughter. Do you want Michelle growing up thinking it's alright for a boy or a man to just beat on her whenever he feels like it? Do you want her having sex with some guy who could be out there having sex with God knows how many different women? Do you remember Sharon Howser, how Mike beat her up just because she asked him to help her get an abortion? What if that was Michelle? Do you know that there are a lot of teenage girls in relationships right now who are being beaten up by their boyfriends? Not just adults, Sara, children as young as thirteen and fourteen years old. Domestic violence is a sickness. It has no age limit and if you're not careful, it can turn into a fatality.

No matter what I say, no matter what anyone says, you are the only person that carries the cure to your domestic violence disease."

"What are you talking about?"

"You'll see one day. Hopefully it won't be too late. Look, change of subject. I've got some great news to tell you. Mama and Tom eloped at the courthouse. They drove down to Fort Lauderdale this morning. Guess what? They are going on a cruise to the Bahamas for their honeymoon. Mama has never gone on a cruise before. I am so excited for her. She is going to have such a good time lying on the beach sipping on a margarita. Isn't it fantastic? Sara, did you hear me? Are you there?"

"Yes, I'm here."

"What's wrong, Sara?"

"I just never thought that Mama would have remarried. I mean, I know that they love each other, but I didn't think they would get married, especially elope. But what about Tom not telling her the truth about him being Mike's brother?"

"Tom is a good man, and you know it."

"Yes I know. I'm happy for Mama. She is a good woman and deserves happiness. At least with Mama being gone on her honeymoon, I won't have to answer any questions about me and Mike."

"Now that's my girl."

"I better get off this phone before Edna overhears us talking."

"You haven't told Edna that you're leaving?"

"Janie, my life for the past eight years has been an absolute nightmare. I can't afford to take any chances that Mike may find out what I'm trying to do."

"Oh, I checked into apartment prices like you asked. You have enough money in your account for at least five months' rent, but you've still got your old room at Mama's house. You and the kids can always come stay with me and Rex. Timmy and Darla have all that extra space out at Tom's old house;

you know that he doesn't mind you living there. Just putting it mildly, little sister, finding a place to stay is your last concern."

"Well, I'll decide what to do when that time comes. Thank you for all of your help. I couldn't do any of this without you and Rex. I'll talk to you later, girl. I've got to head down to the Henderson School Board in an hour to get Michelle switched over to a Loxley elementary school. I'll talk to you later."

"Give the kids a big kiss for me. I love you, Sara. Be careful."

As much as I loved talking to Janie, there was definitely too much on my schedule today.

I couldn't afford to put off my big speech any longer. I was gonna miss Carla. She was a great secretary.

"Good morning, Carla."

"Good morning, Miss Sara."

"Did you put out the memos for the meeting?"

"Yes, ma'am. I did that bright and early this morning. As a matter of fact, the ladies are all waiting for you in the employee break room."

"Thank you, Carla."

A long slow walk to the break room. Although I saw these ladies every day, today would be the hardest and the most important day of my life. As I hesitantly walked into the break room, confidence was definitely not my friend. I had no idea what to say to these ladies. Strength, don't fail me now, I thought. The closer I got to the room, the more nervous I became.

"Ladies, how are you today?"

"We're fine," Edna said, looking surprised. "We all got a memo this morning saying that you needed to see us all in the break room at eleven o'clock. What's going on?"

I stood at the head of the table, fighting off the tears before I even began to speak. "Ladies, I know you all are wondering why I called you together in the middle of the day. I will definitely keep this short and sweet. When I was a little girl, all I ever imagined was life on a farm. The only fantasy I had was having the perfect family. A career or a profession, that's not something I even thought about. I guess I thought I would always do something dealing with agriculture or the environment.

"If anyone had told me seven years ago that I would be an assistant manager for a fashion store, I would have thought they were crazy," I went on. "Although most of you all feel that Henderson is a small town, to me it's a pretty big city. Wearing beautiful clothes and designer shoes, this is all a dream come true for Sara Farraday. Do you know that it took me a year to learn how to walk in those high heels—oh, I'm sorry, I mean stilettos? Thank you. Thank all of you wonderful ladies. I have grown to love you not just as employees, but also as my family."

Darn it, the tears were building up inside of my eyes.

"Sara, what are you trying to say?" Edna asked.

"Edna, please let her finish," Lisa said.

"What I'm saying is that I have enjoyed working here in Henderson with all of you, but the time has come for me and my children to move on."

"Sara, no."

"Edna I especially want to thank you for being not only a good friend, but also a second mother. As of this moment, I am resigning my position as assistant manager. I would like to recommend Lisa Connelly for this position. Lisa and I have become close, and I feel that she is more than capable of handling this position at Edna's Fashions. It's so hard for me to stand here fighting back the tears because I want to cry so badly. I love you all from the bottom of my heart, and I will miss you all. I'll be in my office packing up my things."

My eyes were overloaded with tears. I couldn't help but leave the break room.

"Sara ,wait." Edna tried to stop me.

"Edna, she has to do this," Lisa said. "She needs to get away from Mike. You know that as well as I do. I love Sara just as much as you do, and I made her a promise that I would take over as assistant manager, if you'll have me, and continue to do a wonderful job. I won't disappoint you. I have to do this for Sara. This is her time to enjoy life. Let her go."

Carla helped me finish packing all of my belongings. I expected to see Edna come through the door at any time, but she didn't. I didn't want to leave, but I knew I needed to get some help for myself. I needed to find out why I was still in love with a man who beats me. As I loaded my car with boxes, I glanced up, and Edna was standing there with that last box in her hands.

"You don't think I was just going to let you get away without saying goodbye, now did you? What gave you the courage? I just never thought the day would come when you would leave Mike Farraday. Why didn't you tell me? I'm sure this isn't something that you just planned this morning."

"Edna, I just don't want to talk about this right now. This is so hard for me. I want to do the right thing, but I'm not sure what the right thing is."

"You're doing the right thing. Trust me."

"But my heart is really hurting."

"Sara, love hurts, but in time you will get over Mike. You deserve so much better. Here, put this box in your car. Carla said that you had to go to the school board; go ahead and get down there before they close. We'll stay in touch. You haven't lost anyone; you've only gained new friends. Now, you get out of here. I'll call you later."

Edna gave me a big hug as if this were the last time we would be seeing each other. My car was packed up. The journey had begun. Fear was only the beginning of how I felt. I knew I must think of my children first. As I stepped into my car and drove off for the last time, my face was flooded with tears. Edna waved goodbye to me as I drove out of the parking lot. The traffic was light as I headed downtown. One more look at beautiful downtown Henderson. Palm trees lining the streets. You could see the boats on the bay overlooking the city. Mama and Tom are probably out there somewhere in the Atlantic on their way to the Bahamas, I thought. That's what I always wanted, a romantic getaway for two with the man of my dreams. I could imagine the two of them sipping margaritas, dancing under the moonlight, making love—no I won't imagine Mama making love. I reached the school board with an hour to do what I needed to do before I picked up the kids.

A few hours later, the kids and I arrived home. I promised them pizza. We were all so excited that I didn't notice Mike lying on the sofa taking a nap. Michelle went running into her room.

"Pizza! Pizza! We're gonna have some pizza!"

Mike jumped up from the sofa. "What the hell is that noise! Can't you see I'm trying to sleep?" Mike went into Michelle's room and grabbed her by the arm. I put Michael Jr. down on the floor and ran toward the children's room. Mike slammed the door and locked it behind him.

"Mike! Mike!" I could hear Michelle crying and screaming. I could hear him hitting her. "Daddy, no, please, Daddy, I won't do it again."

"What the hell is wrong with you, running in this damn house, keeping up all of that noise! Don't you see I'm trying to sleep?"

"Mike, please don't hurt her. Mike, don't hurt her!" All of a sudden the door opened. Mike walked out of the room and grabbed me by my arm.

"You better keep both of them quiet, or I'll beat you next."

He walked into our bedroom and slammed the door. Michelle was lying on her bed crying. She had her hand over her mouth so that Mike wouldn't hear her. I looked at her legs. They were fiery red. Mike had hit her legs with his hand.

"Mommy, I'm sorry. I didn't know that Daddy was trying to take a nap. I won't do it again, Mommy, I promise."

I couldn't help but cry myself. But it gave me great comfort in knowing that he would never put his hand on one of my children again. We all stayed in the room together. A couple of hours later, Mike came banging on the children's door.

"What is it, Mike?"

"Can you please open the door, honey?"

"Mommy, I'm scared."

"It's alright, Michelle. You and your brother just stay there on the bed. Do you understand? Just keep Michael Jr. in here with you. When I walk out of this room, lock the door behind me, OK?"

"Yes, Mommy."

I opened the door and slowly stepped out of the room, closing the door behind me. "Did you need something, Mike?"

Mike mocked my every word. "Did you need something, Mike? Yes, I'd like to get some dinner, if that's alright with you, Sara honey? What happened to the pizza? Didn't you order some pizza for your kids?"

"No. I didn't."

"And why not?"

"Michelle lost her appetite after you hit her."

"Is Michelle the only person that has to eat around here? Do I need to go back in there and hit her again in order to get something to eat?"

"There is some beef stew in the refrigerator. All you have to do is heat it up in the microwave?"

Before I could finish talking, Mike walked over to me and hit me in the stomach with his fist.

"No, Sara! You heat it up! I'm so sick and tired of your smart mouth. You're my wife. You get in that kitchen and heat it up." Mike took the belt out of his pants. "I see what you need. You need a good old-fashioned beating."

Mike hit me at least six or seven times across my back with his belt. "Mike, please, I'm going to the kitchen, please just give me time to heat up your food. Don't hit me anymore, please."

I moved as fast as I could, desperately not trying to make Mike any more upset than he already was. I didn't want the children to hear me screaming. I prayed that they wouldn't open the bedroom door. Mike already had a plate of beef stew in the refrigerator from yesterday. I got the plate out and heated it up in the microwave. Mike put his belt back into his pants. My back felt like someone had just poured a bucket of scalding hot water on it. I was in so much pain that I bit down on my bottom lip to keep from screaming out.

"Now, that's the way a wife should treat her man."

I put the plate on the kitchen table. Mike just looked at it. "You know what? I don't think I want any beef stew after all. I'm going to work. A Billy burger sounds pretty good right now. Why don't you clean up this entire mess, babe? I'll see you later."

Mike walked over to me and kissed me on my cheek just before walking out of the front door. I was in so much pain that I fell down to the floor.

"Mommy, Mommy, are you alright?"

"Don't touch Mommy right now, Michelle."

"Do I need to call nine one one?" Michelle asked.

"No. Call Aunt Janie and tell her and Uncle Rex to come over to the house. Tell him to bring his truck. Their phone number is in the red book next to the phone. Michelle, I want you to help me in the bathroom. Michael Jr., Mommy wants you to go in your room and put all of your toys in the toy chest."

"Mommy, Aunt Janie wants to talk to you."

" Hey, Janie."

"What the hell is going on there? Michelle is crying. What did that bastard do, Sara?"

"Janie, listen to me. I don't want anymore problems. Just send Rex and one of the other guys to help get our things just like we planned."

"Do I need to call the police?"

"No, I don't even want you to come. Just send Rex and Peter. We don't have that much stuff. They can probably load up everything at one time, and I'll put everything else in my car. I'm sending Michelle back with them. Can you watch her for me tonight?"

"Aren't you coming too?"

"No, I can't. The school board won't release Michelle's paperwork until tomorrow."

"Won't she be missing her last day of school?"

"She's taken all her tests and completed everything. I'll go by the school and give them her new address for them to send her grades."

"I'll take care of her. What about Michael Jr.? Is he coming with them?"

"I don't think so. You know how he likes to stay close to his mommy. I can take him to school until I'm finished doing everything that I need to do. We can drive down to Loxley tomorrow evening."

"Are you sure? You still didn't tell me why Michelle was crying."

"Yes, Janie, I'm sure. Look, instead of us talking, can you send Rex down to Henderson for those boxes, please, ma'am?"

"I'm sorry. Sure, I'll tell him to head that way right now, little sister. Just be patient. It's almost over. I met a good-looking lawyer who said he could handle your divorce."

"Oh, really."

"I think you even know him. He says that the two of you went to school together."

Oh, Janie, I don't feel like talking right now, I thought. I've got to look at my back.

"His name is Evan Slade."

"That name does sound familiar, but the Evan Slade I remember wasn't that good-looking."

"Well, guess what, Sara honey: it's amazing what contact lenses and a five hundred dollar suit can do for you. I've got to go hunt Rex. I'll talk with you later, girl."

"Good-bye."

"Mommy, you didn't tell her what happened."

"Trust me, Michelle, it would have only made matters worse. We're gonna play a game. We are going to be nurses taking care of each other. I'm gonna put this cream on your legs and you are going to put this cream on Mommy's back, alright? Let's get started."

Michelle and I went into my bedroom and put antibiotic cream on each other. Oh my goodness did that feel better. The places on my back weren't as bad as I thought they were. Michelle said she felt better also. We both went into the kids' room. Michelle packed up her clothes, and I packed up Michael Jr.'s clothes. Mike had never come home this early, so we had a pretty good chance of getting everything packed and out of there. I wanted to kill him for what he did to Michelle. She is one of the most beautiful children. I have never had to punish Michelle for anything and couldn't stand the thought of him taking out his anger on her. I just had to get her out of this house tonight.

We packed for at least three hours before Rex and Peter showed up. We were really moving. I was glad that Mike never looks in my car. There were several boxes that I had been packing up each day. Rex and Peter took down the children's beds and placed them on the truck, along with all of their toys and clothes. I only took what I brought to the house—television sets, the computer, and a DVD player for the kids. Plus the pots and pans, some of the old antique pictures that were on the living room wall, just some things that Mike never noticed and often took for granted.

"Rex, I think we've got everything that we need. I've got most of the clothes and shoes in my car. That's everything."

"Sara, I've noticed that you've been limping since Peter and I got here. I also noticed that little Michelle's legs are awfully red and swollen. Mike did something. I know that you're not gonna admit it, but I can tell that he has been beating on the both of you. Why don't you let Peter and I go find his ass and beat the hell out of him? Just this once. No one has to know what happened. We won't even tell Janie about any of this. I can't stand that jerk. I got drunk once a long time ago, and thought I was gonna hit Janie just to prove to the guys that I was a big man. Hell, I ain't embarrassed to say she darn near whooped my ass.

But it taught me a lesson. I will respect Janie and any other woman for the rest of my life. Women aren't punching bags for men to take their anger out on, and Mike has a lot of anger inside. Are you sure you don't want to call the police?"

"I can't call the police, Rex. When I testified for Mike, I lied under oath. Mike said that if I ever called the police again, he would tell the judge what I did and the courts would take away my kids."

"That son of a dog. We better get this truck on the road. Where are you going to stay tonight?"

"I want you to take Michelle back to Loxley with you."

"What about Michael Jr.?"

"You can forget it. He already said he wants to stay with Mommy. I can handle him. We are going to spend the night at Edna and Joe's. I've got a ten o'clock appointment at the school board, then I have to go by Henderson Elementary and give them a new address for Michelle. Do you mind if I use your address?"

"No, don't be silly. I'm gonna take your stuff to our house and set it up in the spare bedroom."

I gave Rex a big hug. He had turned out to be more than just a brother-in-law. He had turned out to be a real friend.

"Michelle, I want you to go with Rex and Peter. You be a good little girl, and I will see you later. Janie is gonna take good care of you."

"Mommy, I'm scared."

"Baby, Daddy is not gonna hurt you ever again."

"I'm not scared for me, I'm scared that something bad is going to happen to you."

"No, baby. Mommy doesn't have to ever go near Daddy again. Trust me. I love you and I'll see you later. Now give me a big kiss."

"She'll be alright, Sara," Rex said. "You take care. See you later."

As they drove off down the street, I strapped Michael Jr. into his car seat and we headed toward Edna's house. I couldn't believe all of this was happening. I thought about leaving a note for Mike. Regardless of everything, I still somehow had feelings for this man. But I had to let it go in order to set some kind of example for my children. It would break my heart to know that Michelle was in a relationship where domestic violence was taking place.

CHAPTER TWENTY-SEVEN:

A Living Nightmare

One o'clock in the morning. Michael Jr. was asleep. "Damn it!" I said out loud. "I can't believe this. I left my purse at the house."

How stupid could I be to forget my own purse. I had to turn around and go get it. As soon as I got my cellphone, I could call Edna and let her know I was on my way. It took twenty minutes for me to drive back to the house.

Mike's car was in the driveway. The house was pitch dark. That was strange. I wondered what in the hell he was doing home so early. It was almost as if he was watching for us to leave, so he could come home. There was an empty space on the street, so I decided to park my car there and walk to the house. As I parked the car, Michael Jr. woke up.

"Mommy, I have to pee."

"Alright, sweetie. Listen to Mommy. I'm gonna let you stand next to the car so that you can pee, alright?" I got out of the car, unfastened MJ's car seat so that he could stand next to the back of the car. "Sweetie, we are gonna go to the back door of the house. Mommy's gonna go inside and get her purse. I need you to be really quiet so that we won't disturb Daddy. Can you do that for Mommy, please?"

"Yes."

Michael Jr. put his head on my shoulder immediately after I picked him up. He was so tired, he fell right back to sleep.

Trying to be extremely quiet, I tiptoed around to the back of the house. The back door was already unlocked. When I turned the knob and opened the door, it was as if no one was at home. Maybe Mike just came back and dropped off his car. I left the back door open to let the outside lights shine into the house. I opened the door to the children's room. My purse was still there where I left it. Desperately tiptoeing in as fast as I could, I grabbed my purse and began to head toward the back door. Just then, I heard some strange sounds. I also noticed flickering lights from underneath our bedroom door. The noise got louder and louder. It sounded like moaning and definitely a man's voice.

"Baby, don't stop. Oh, yeah. Don't stop. That feels so good, baby."

That was Mike's voice. Who was he talking to? All of a sudden, I heard a loud scream coming from the bedroom. I hesitantly walked to the door. Gently turning the knob, the door slowly opened. Oh my goodness, what I saw inside that room was something that I will never forget as long as I live. Mike was having anal sex with Chris in our bed. Both of them were naked. Chris was on his hands and knees in the bed wearing a long red wig, and Mike was straddling him from behind. I couldn't believe what I was seeing. My husband was having sex with a man in our bed. Mike got up, putting on his pants when he noticed I was standing at the door.

"Sara, what the hell are you doing here? The neighbors called me and said they saw you hauling your stuff out of here about an hour ago! Why did you come back?"

"What neighbors, Mike?"

"Bobby Harris, the fireman that lives across the street. Yeah, he's one of my best customers at the club. He buys at least three girls a week. He told me that you had some guys here in a truck packing up your stuff. I figured I'd just be a gentleman and let you get what you wanted so you could get out of here."

"Mike, you are having sex with a man in our bedroom."

"Well, I'm sorry you had to see that, but you weren't supposed to be here."

Chris jumped out of bed and ran into the bathroom with embarrassment written all over his face.

"Wait a minute. Chris. That's the woman, I mean the man, who came here to the house that day looking for his two thousand dollars."

"Yeah, we got that situation straightened out, just a little lovers quarrel."

I could feel myself getting nauseated with every word that Mike spoke. My head felt so light. I ran into the living room. After I laid Michael Jr. on the sofa, I quickly went toward the bathroom in the hallway, vomiting everywhere. My insides felt if though they had been ripped out. All the while I was thinking, how could this creep do this to me? I stayed in the bathroom for at least thirty minutes. Thank goodness, Michael Jr. didn't wake up to see his father sticking his penis into another man's butt.

"Sara. Sara. Are you alright?"

"No, I'm not alright, Mike." I grabbed a towel and washed my face. "You are going to give me some answers, Mike Farraday."

"Well, it's pretty simple. It all started when I was a little boy. Oh...Should I lie on the couch while I explain myself to you?"

Tears were rolling down my face. My eyes were blood red. I was so angry, I could feel my own heart beating.

"Look Sara. When I was a little boy, I hated the fact that I didn't have a mother. The man that I thought was my grandfather wanted me to be just like him. I didn't want to be like him. He taught me everything there was to know about a horse. He didn't want me to have any friends or anything, all he wanted was for me to grow up in his image. I hated that old man.

"One night I went out to the stables at Tom's ranch," Mike went on. "There was a ranch hand there by the name of Thomas French. He had a son named Christopher. He told me to call him Chris, because he hated his real name. That same night when I went to the stables to check on the horses like

Granddaddy Farraday told me to, I saw Chris. I didn't know what he was doing at first, but when I got close to him, I could see that he was masturbating while looking in a *Playgirl* magazine. Oh, man, I couldn't believe what I was seeing. As I walked toward him, he stopped.

"Something happened to me that night. We both began to touch each other. I was thirteen years old. Man, did it feel good. I heard the old man yelling my name. He came down to the stables to look for me, but instead, he found two naked little boys giving each other oral sex. He grabbed his chest and ran off toward the main house. They found my granddaddy dead, sitting in the living room the next morning. The doctors said that he had a heart attack in his sleep. Chris and I knew what killed him, but we never told anyone. I felt a little guilty and decided not to go to his funeral, but I thought that would have made Tom and nosy Aunt Edna suspicious, so I decided to just show up at the gravesite.

"As I was walking toward my family, I overheard them saying that granddaddy was my real father. He had been screwing around with my mom and got her pregnant. Tom had been sterile since he was a teenager. I was pissed off for a while, but what the hell, nothing would have been any different no matter who was my father."

Mike shrugged his shoulders. "I figured since they kept the secret from me, I'd keep the secret from them. I treated Tom like it was his fault. It all worked out. Tom gave me Granddaddy's old red Mustang. He gave me money. I didn't have to explain anything; he just gave me whatever I wanted. So I decided I'd keep treating Tom like dirt, that way I could get whatever I wanted. The only problem was, Chris's father got a job in Henderson. They moved away. I would sneak down to see him every once in a while, but he started hanging with other guys and dressing like a girl, that was just a little bit to much for me to deal with."

"What about all those girls, like Sharon Howser? She was pregnant with your child."

"Wait a minute. I didn't say that I didn't like women. I love women, but sometimes I feel comfortable being with someone that understands me. Every once in a while, I find myself being attracted to a man. As far as Sharon Howser was concerned, she was never pregnant. I used a condom with every girl I ever had sex with, except you."

"I don't understand. You told me Sharon was pregnant."

"I lied! That stupid little whore snuck into my house one day and caught me and James Parker in a compromising position. She got pissed off and threatened to tell the coach and the other football players. I offered her money, my car, everything I could think of, but she still said she was going to tell what she had seen. James and I drove her out by the old Hawthorne place. We tried to scare her into not telling anybody, but she got mad and slapped me across the face. She hit me so hard, that her fingernails scratched my cheek.

"I was upset," he continued. "It's like I just started hitting her and I couldn't stop. It's as if I saw everything bad that ever happened to me in her eyes. She was no longer Sharon Howser, she was something evil and I had to protect myself. After hitting her several times, she finally fell on the ground. James told me she wasn't breathing. For a minute I got scared. We decided to rip her shirt and just leave her there on the ground. A couple of days later, some of the kids at school started talking about how she had been found by two old farmers. They drove her to the hospital. James and I went to see if the stories were true. She didn't remember what happened, at least that's what she told everyone. That's when James and I came up with the story about her being pregnant."

Mike looked at me with fire in his eyes.

"You know, you women are crazy. Do you know that I got more attention from girls after they thought I had beat up Sharon? Even you. You thought it was sexy and cool that Mike Farraday beat up his ex-girlfriend, didn't you? Now I could pay more attention to little homely pathetic Sara Ramsey. The farm girl that no one wanted."

"You told me that you used a condom every time that we had sex."

"Well, guess what, honey? I lied again! I never used a condom. Don't you understand? I wanted you to get pregnant."

"What are you talking about?"

"It's all about this house. I knew that Tom had the hots for your mama and if you got pregnant, he would want me to marry you. Tom is a true gentleman, I must admit. Maybe one day when I grow up, I'll be just like him."

Mike started to laugh uncontrollably, like some kind of madman.

"The house, Sara. My father left this house to Tom when he died. Tom promised me, once I got married and had a family of my own, I could have the house. That's why I needed your help. We had to get married and move to Henderson. Chris called me and said Billy was making a lot of money at his club. I knew right then and there that Big Billy needed a partner. There was just one problem, I had to be twenty-one years old. That's where good old Uncle Joe came on the scene. Tom talked him into getting me a job at the coal mine. Two years of suffering in that hellhole, but it was worth it, in order to make a thousand dollars a week. Girl, that is some good money. Did I mention it was tax-free money? Sara, Sara, Sara."

Mike started rubbing my face. "Don't put your hands on me," I said.

"Oh, baby girl. Don't act like that."

Chris walked by toward the front door. "Hey, where do you think you're going?"

"I'm out of here, Mike. You've got a situation to handle. I'll see you later."

"Chris, wait."

Chris walked out the house and slammed the front door behind him.

"I'm getting out of here too," I said. "You are a sick man, Mike Farraday. I don't believe you beat me like a damn dog, just so you could have a house."

"No. I beat you because you deserved it. That was your fault, not mine."

"You're not even sorry for what you put me and my kids through, are you?"

"That was your fault. You have no one to blame but yourself."

"Alright, Mike, you can have this house and everything in it, but I'm not gonna let you get away with what you did to me and my children."

"What are you gonna do? Call the police? Yeah, why don't you do that, so I can tell the judge how you lied in his courtroom. You can't prove I did anything."

"I'm not gonna call the police. I'm gonna tell Tom and Edna how you watched your own father have a heart attack and didn't say a word about it. You could have saved his life if you would have called an ambulance. You and Chris watched him die. I'm gonna tell them what he saw in those stables the last night of his life. I'm gonna tell everyone back in Loxley what a sick freak you are. How you beat your wife for years just because you were too afraid to come to terms with your own sexuality. I'll put an ad in the newspaper if I have too, but I won't let you get away with what you did to me. You're nothing but a stupid drunk. I can smell the alcohol on your breath."

Mike started to walk toward me, sweat dropping off his face. His eyes were fiery red. He grabbed me by the neck.

"Shut up! No, I'm gonna shut you up for good, Sara."

With both hands around my neck, he continued to push me until my back was against the kitchen sink, choking every ounce of air out of my body. I couldn't breath. I thought he was going to kill me for sure.

All of a sudden, Mike started to yell. He finally let go of my neck. Michael Jr. had wandered into the kitchen and bit Mike on the back of his leg. Mike was filled with so much anger and rage, he turned around and slapped Michael Jr. as hard as he could. I finally got my breath, but by that time it was to late.

Michael Jr. had accidentally hit the back of his head on the kitchen table. My baby was lying on the floor with a pool of blood underneath his head.

"Mike what have you done?" I screamed at him.

Mike tried to come after me again, but I grabbed a knife that was lying on the kitchen counter. I cut the top of his hand, and I was prepared to kill him if he didn't let me get to my son. Mike grabbed his hand and was steadily yelling how all of this was my fault. I knelt down beside Michael Jr. His little chest was barely moving. There was so much blood on the floor.

Within seconds the police kicked open the front door. Mike told the police that it was all my fault. He even accused me of trying to kill him. The ambulance arrived shortly afterward and took Michael Jr. to the hospital. I rode along with them. The police took Mike to jail. I sat in Michael Jr.'s hospital room until the police came and arrested me also.

CHAPTER TWENTY-EIGHT:

A Deadly Ending

My twenty-one days in jail went by like an eternity. Then out of the blue, I received a visit from Mama, Tom, and my lawyer. This was the best day of my life. They came to tell me that all the charges had been dropped and I was free to leave the jail. But the best news of all, Mama told me that Michael Jr. was awake and was calling for me. As soon as my paperwork was processed, we all drove over to the hospital. I ran faster than I had ever run before. There he was, my little angel.

"Hello, little man."

I wanted to hold on to my little boy and never let go. "Mommy, I missed you, Mommy."

"I missed you too, Michael. Mommy will never leave you again. Doctor, can you tell us what happened? My mother said that he didn't need the surgery?"

"Your son is a strong little boy. He's also something of a miracle as well. When the swelling of his brain went down, the injury that had occurred simply healed itself."

"But what about all of the blood that I saw on the floor?"

"It came from the laceration that he sustained when he hit his head. That simply means that he cut his head on a sharp part of the table. We had to put in some stitches, but that area is healing just fine. By him being in that medically induced coma., his body was able to do a great deal of healing on its own. Like I said, Mrs. Farraday, your son is a strong little boy."

"Can I take him home?"

"We want to keep him for at least another forty-eight hours. Then if there are no problems, you can take him home."

Everything seemed to be working out well. That eternity I spent in jail was worth it, just to see my little boy alive and well again.

Everyone in the family had come to visit. The hospital room was filled with people. Mama, Tom, Edna, Joe, Janie, Rex, Timmy, Peter, and my other little angel, Michelle. Janie said she had taken care of transferring Michelle to Loxley Elementary. Timmy decided that the kids and I could stay in the guest-house on Tom's old ranch. Mama was a little disappointed that I refused to live with her and Tom. I felt that since they were newlyweds, they needed their privacy and their own space. My lawyer, Steven Jones, had been my rock through all of this. He was also working on my divorce.

"I don't believe it," I said. "In two days I can take my son home and start to live my new life. I'm just so glad that Mike is finally gonna go to prison for everything that he's put us through."

"I'm not so sure about that, Sara," Steven replied. "I didn't want to mention it to you, but I think you all need to know. Mike was released from jail about a week ago on bond. I'm not sure when his trial is coming up. Sara, I am so sorry."

My heart felt as though it had literally stopped beating. I couldn't say a word.

"How in the hell is he out there walking around free?" Janie asked. "He almost killed his son and his wife. What is wrong with that judge?"

"Have you seen him lately, Tom?" Julia asked.

"Julia, I've washed my hands of Mike. He's on his own. He shouldn't be out there walking the streets free. This is ridiculous."

"I know that Mike is my nephew, but something bad is going to happen to him," Joe said. "He's hurt too many people."

"Sara, are you alright? You're just sitting there." Julia said.."

"I'm alright. Michael Jr. is getting pretty tired, you guys."

"Yeah, we all need to leave and let him get some rest. Sara, do you want to come to Edna's house with me and get a shower and a good night's sleep?"

"No, Mama, I'll take a shower once Michael Jr. falls off to sleep. I'll just sit in the recliner next to his bed. I just want to make sure he's alright."

"Well, the rest of us are gonna head back to Loxley and get everything fixed up for you and the kids."

"I'm gonna stay here in Henderson with you, Sara, and as soon as MJ is discharged, we can ride back to Loxley in my car," mama said.

"Thank you, Mama."

Mama kissed me on my forehead. "Get you some rest. I'll see you tomorrow, baby. Bye, Michael Jr."

After everyone left the hospital, I took a nice hot shower. That felt like heaven. When I came out of the bathroom, Michael Jr. was asleep. I kissed him good night and sat in the chair next to his bed. I was exhausted. I couldn't get the idea out of my head that Michael Farraday was somewhere out there walking around. It wasn't right.

The day had finally come for Michael Jr. to be released from the hospital. I opened my eyes around three in the morning. My body was stiff and aching from sleeping in that recliner chair for two nights. I couldn't wait to sleep in a real bed. He had done so well the past two days.

A few hours later, I was awakened by Mama and Tom's voice. "Sara, Sara. Honey, are you alright?"

"Mama, Tom. What time is it?"

"It's seven thirty. The nurse is here with Michael Jr.'s breakfast. Have you seen the news this morning?"

"No, ma'am. I was trying to sleep. Wow, this chair can be uncomfortable after sleeping in it for a few hours."

"Sweetheart let's step outside the door for a minute. What is that on your shoe?"

"I don't know,"

"It looks like dried mud, sweetie."

"Oh, I forgot, I went outside last night for a walk. This chair had my body so stiff; I decided to walk around the hospital for a few minutes while Michael Jr. was asleep."

"I am so sorry to be the one to tell you this, but the police found Mike's body this morning behind the Dumpster at Billy's Lounge. Sara, he's dead."

"Dead? What happened to him, Mama?"

"The police said that his throat had been cut," Tom replied. "It happened sometime in the last twenty-four hours."

"Did the police call you in Loxley to tell you what had happened, Tom?"

"No, Sara, I never left Henderson. I wanted to stick around here and make sure that you and your mother got back home safely when the hospital released Michael Jr."

Suddenly, another voice interrupted our conversation.

"Excuse me, Mrs. Farraday. I don't know if you remember me or not. My name is Detective O'Hara."

"Yes, Detective, I remember you very well."

"Mrs. Farraday, I would like to apologize for arresting you that night for what happened to your son. We knew that your husband was lying about everything, but we have laws that we have to follow, ma'am."

"Please, Detective, don't call me ma'am. It makes me sick when you all call me ma'am. Why are you here? I was cleared of all of the charges, and I know that you're not here because you're interested in my son's condition. So, why are you here?"

"Ma'am, I mean Mrs. Farraday, I'm not sure if you're aware or not, but your husband's body was found this morning by some sanitation workers. He was lying next to the Dumpster in the alley behind Big Billy's Lounge. Forensics said he's probably been there anywhere from twenty-four to forty-eight hours. His throat was cut."

"Detective, do you all have any evidence as to who might have done this to Mike?" Tom asked.

"No, but the crime scene was pretty clean."

"What do you mean by clean?"

"It seems if though your son didn't put up a struggle at all. His fingernails were clean. There was so sign of a fight. Usually in those cases it leads us to believe that the victim knew the suspect very well. Actually, well enough to allow him or her to get close enough to him to cut his throat. We'll know more after the autopsy. There were some footprints, but I've been told that area is pretty well known for drug trafficking.

"Mrs. Farraday, I hate to ask you this, especially right now, but do you know of anyone who might have threatened your husband when the two of you were together?"

Why is this guy in my face asking me all of these stupid questions, I wondered. Maybe I should tell him about Tina and what she said would happen to Mike when her old man got out of prison. No, I would let the police earn their money and figure it out for themselves.

I don't know anything about Mike's life. Maybe he and Chris had a lovers quarrel. Oh…Forget this guy. I just wanted to go back to Loxley and start my new life.

"Detective, Mike never talked about his job," I said. "To be honest, we didn't talk about much of anything. He didn't mention anyone threatening him."

"Sara, there's the doctor." Tom said. "Good morning, everyone."

"Good morning, Dr. Johnson," we replied.

"Sara, I was just on the way to tell you that we just got the results of the last MRI on your son, and everything looks good. All of his bloodwork is normal. He hasn't had any fever in the last forty-eight hours. Your son is ready to go home. How does that sound? I'm sorry. I feel like I just interrupted something."

"No, Dr. Johnson, you didn't interrupt," Mama said. "My son-in-law was killed, and they found his body this morning. The detective wanted to come by and ask Sara some questions."

"Sir, you should not be in this hospital," the doctor said. "Mrs. Farraday has been here for the last two days by her son's bedside hoping and praying for his recovery. Now, I am sorry for what happened to her husband, but if it had not been for him, her son would not be lying in that bed. That woman has been in jail for a crime she did not commit. Please, just let her go home in peace and live her life with her children. Sir, I'm gonna have to ask you to leave the building. Sara needs to prepare her son for their trip home."

"I do apologize again, Mrs. Farraday. Please do me one favor; just stop by the police station and leave us a phone number where we can reach you, just in case we get any new leads about your husband's death."

"I'll stop by the police station with a number where we can be reached," Tom replied.

"You all have a good day," the detective said. "I'm sorry for you and your family's loss, Mrs. Farraday. Here's my card, just in case you think of something later that may help with the investigation."

As Detective Stupid walked away, I was so glad that he didn't notice the mud on my shoes. He probably wouldn't have believed me if I told him I went for a walk around the hospital last night because I couldn't sleep. Thank goodness no one noticed but Mama and Tom. I didn't mention anything to Mama, but I noticed when I glanced down at Tom's shoes, they were covered with mud.

We all went into Michael Jr.'s room. The nurse had given him his bath and put on his cloths. Dr. Johnson had just finished his discharge papers. I couldn't believe it, but we were ready to leave Henderson. Tom went down to drive the car around to the front of the hospital. The caretaker took Michael Jr. down the elevator in a wheelchair. Mama and I were so happy. We carried all the toys and gifts that he had received since he had been in the hospital for nearly a month.

We all got in the car and drove off toward Loxley. Michael Jr. was still a little groggy from the medication. He went back to sleep. Tom said he would call the Henderson Police Station and give them his phone number once he got me and MJ home to rest.

"Tom, aren't you going to stop at the Henderson Police Station before we leave for Loxley?" Mama asked.

"No, Julia. I'll call the good detective when I get home. The real estate office gave me a call. It seems as though Mike was planning on selling the house. I never told my dear brother, but I signed over the house to Sara and any children that she may have. So Sara, legally the house is still yours. I know that you were planning on moving back to Loxley, so I had a talk with your neighbors. Ms. Abigail's great-niece and her family are planning on moving to Henderson next month. I told them that if they are interested, I'm sure you'd be willing to sell them the house for a little bit of nothing."

"Thanks, Tom. I appreciate you handling that situation for me. You know, that's all he wanted was the house. The kids and I were merely the insurance that went along with it."

"That idea did cross my mind a few times. Mike just wasn't the responsible type. I really did believe that he would be willing to change once he found the right person to share his life with. That was my mistake, and I am so sorry for the hell you had to go through."

"No, Tom. I really and truly loved Mike, but I hated the sickness that dwelled within him."

"Do you think that friend of his might have something to do with his death, Tom?" Mama asked.

"Mike was into so many different things, there is no telling who killed him. Joe said the guys at the coal mine told him that Mike had teenagers selling drugs for him at schools and on street corners. He was pimping out prostitutes, males and females as young as fifteen years old. He beat up several of the ladies who worked at the club. Do you believe he shot at some of the women? Joe told me a lot of sick things about Mike. Some of them, I can't bear to repeat right now. It just hurts my heart to know that my brother did all of those terrible things."

Tears started to roll down Tom's face. "I promised I wouldn't do this."

"Tom, there's nothing wrong with crying," Mama said. "Although Mike wasn't the best person in the world, he was still your brother and you loved him."

"Evidently my little brother liked to do a lot of boasting about how he kept the ladies in line. Sara, I hope you don't hate me for saying this, but whoever killed Mike did him a favor. He had a one-way ticket to destruction. I'm just glad that you and the kids didn't end up going with him."

"So am I, Tom. So am I."

The drive didn't take long at all. When we arrived at the ranch, Michelle came running toward the car. I had missed my little girl. I think I spent the first few days just crying out of sheer happiness. It felt so good to be safe with my little angels. The kids and I loved the guesthouse. There were three huge bedrooms, a kitchen, living room, and a den.

We all had to make another trip back to Henderson for Mike's funeral. He had been so busy enjoying his wonderful life that he didn't take the time to purchase any insurance on himself, but I did. He probably thought that he would live forever. I saw the path that Mike was going down. I had taken out a four hundred thousand dollar policy on him seven years ago. Since the good Dr. Johnson had already told Detective O'Hara that I was with Michael Jr. for two days, no one questioned why I took out such a huge policy on my husband. The good doctor didn't realize it, but he gave me the perfect alibi.

We had a small graveside service. I cried at the funeral. I wasn't crying over his death, I was crying over the way he wasted his life. Such a young man. Died before he was even thirty years old. I expected to see Chris lurking around in the shadows or hiding behind a tree, but he wasn't there. The children didn't want to go to the funeral, but I wanted them to go. I didn't want them growing up with the guilt of not attending their father's funeral, like Mike had to deal with for so many years.

While I was in Henderson, the kids and I got a chance to say good-bye to the Peck sisters. I sold the house to their great niece and her husband. They seemed like a nice couple. It was nice of her to want to move to Henderson to take care of her great-aunts. Everyone got a chance to say good-bye to Joe and Edna also. Edna decided to sell her store to some buyers from New York, with the terms that they keep the same employees. They bought a condo in Miami two miles from their daughter. Joe retired from the coal mine. I think the two of them couldn't face living in a city where Mike was killed. People asking questions every day. They both wanted to retire to find some peace of mind.

Edna was nice enough to give me a third of the money that she received from selling the store. I told her that she didn't have to do that, but she insisted. The shop had made so much progress in the last six years. It was time for its name to be known all over the world, not just in some parts of Florida. Everything was finally taken care of in Henderson. I left without turning back.

A few months later, we had settled into the guesthouse. The kids loved it there. Mama's barn was a few blocks down the road. They could go there and visit her and Tom whenever they wanted to. Rex continued to show them how to ride the horses. I was what you would call a stay-at-home mom. Tom introduced me to the investment world. I used some of the money that I received from Mike's insurance policy. The money seemed to pretty much double itself in a matter of months.

I also attended counseling three times a week. At first it was hard, but when I walked in that room and heard all of those woman and men talking about how they had been in abusive relationships, all I could do was cry. For so long, I just didn't believe that so many people had been through the same things that I had gone through. I was ashamed to tell anyone. Most importantly, I was afraid to even believe it myself. It was so much easier just waking up every day pretending that everything was going to be alright, he would get better soon, and I would finally have the man of my dreams. All I did was force myself to believe in a lie. I suffered from a disease known as domestic violence.

I was one of the lucky ones because my children and I made it out alive. Many women aren't so lucky. They would rather live in denial than deal with the facts staring them in the face every day of their lives. I know it will take some time, but I will overcome my feelings for Mike and move on with my life, if not for my sake, then for the love of my beautiful children.

My lawyer, Stephen, came down to Loxley and finalized my divorce.

He was a nice man. We occasionally went out to dinner. He would stop by the ranch and spend time with the kids. I wasn't looking to get into a relationship right now, but it was nice to have the company of a nice man around every once in a while. He also kept me informed about any news concerning Mike's death.

The police still hadn't found any suspects. Like Tom said, Mike lived a terrible life. Anyone could have come after him. Maybe Mike decided to dump his lover Chris for someone else or started to steal his money again. Joe and Edna did all of a sudden decide that they wanted to leave Henderson; maybe they were trying to get away from something that they didn't want anyone to know about. Rex, Timmy, and Peter said they drove back to Loxley that night. Maybe they took a detour first and decided to go by and check out Big Billy's Lounge before leaving Henderson. Tina's old man, as she called him, was due to get out of prison soon. I think she did mention something about him stabbing someone before in the past. Tom was pretty upset about Mike's behavior and he did have mud on the side of his shoes. Joe probably told him that Mike was bisexual. Tom, being the man that he was, may have felt that Mike needed to be put out of his misery.

I had suffered at Mike's hands for eight years. This man had almost killed my child, and then he was out walking around free. The judge didn't care. The police didn't care. Maybe I had decided to seek my own revenge. No…not a homely, pathetic little farm girl like Sara Farraday.

Made in the USA
Middletown, DE
03 October 2017